Waking Merlin

Tanya Landman has been part of Storybox Theatre since 1992, working as a writer, administrator and performer – a job which has taken her to festivals all over the world. *Waking Merlin* is Tanya's first book. She says, "One morning I got out of bed and said aloud (for no apparent reason), 'Katrina Picket'. The first sentence of *Waking Merlin* dropped into my head, and the rest of the book followed very quickly. In the first year I started writing books, I was like an uncorked champagne bottle – the ideas positively exploded!" Tanya is also the author of *Merlin's Apprentice*, the second Katrina Picket adventure, and *Flotsam and Jetsam*, a modern fairytale for confident young readers. She lives with her family in Devon.

Another Katrina Picket adventure
Merlin's Apprentice

Other books by the same author
Flotsam and Jetsam

Waking Merlin

TANYA LANDMAN

Illustrated by THOMAS TAYLOR

WALKER
BOOKS

This is a work of fiction. Names, characters, places and incidents are
either the product of the author's imagination or, if real, are used fictitiously.

First published 2005 by Walker Books Ltd
87 Vauxhall Walk, London SE11 5HJ

This edition published 2006

2 4 6 8 10 9 7 5 3 1

Text © 2005 Tanya Landman
Illustrations © 2005 Thomas Taylor

The right of Tanya Landman and Thomas Taylor to be identified as author
and illustrator respectively of this work has been asserted by them in
accordance with the Copyright, Designs and Patents Act 1988

This book has been typeset in Stempel Schneidler

Printed and bound in Great Britain
by Creative Print and Design (Wales), Ebbw Vale

British Library Cataloguing in Publication Data:
a catalogue record for this book
is available from the British Library

ISBN-13: 978-1-4063-0250-9
ISBN-10: 1-4063-0250-3

www.walkerbooks.co.uk

For Rod: for believing that I could;
for Isaac and Jack:
for putting up with me while I did;
and for Mum: for laughing in all the right places

Potholes
(Friday morning)

When she was ten years old, Katrina Picket woke Merlin. It was quite by accident – she'd had no intention of doing any such thing. But it was fortunate for everyone in England that she did.

They didn't know, of course. The whole thing had to be hushed up. Most people thought it was a particularly inventive party for the Queen's jubilee. And as for the dragon and the exploding fireball – they were explained away as impressive special effects.

But Katrina, and the Prime Minister, knew different.

* * *

The long summer holidays had just started. It was Dad's idea of a fun day out to take Katrina potholing in the Mendips. He was fond of what most people called "dangerous sports". Katrina had already refused to go rock climbing with him because she was scared of heights. But potholing sounded safer, somehow. Katrina imagined cosy tunnels and warm underground burrows.

The thought of it had been quite exciting.

The reality was not.

It was cold, it was dark, it was wet and it was scary. Water oozed down cave walls that were covered in sinister-looking slime. Strange mud collected in puddles that had to be crawled through. The torches on their safety helmets cast weird shadows: faces seemed to leer from the rocks just out of Katrina's line of vision, only to disappear every time she turned to look at them. Tiny claustrophobic tunnels opened out into vast caves, where terrifying ravines gaped in the blackness. It was exactly like rock climbing, thought Katrina as they edged round a particularly nasty chasm and squeezed into another tunnel. Rock climbing in the dark.

Underground. Where you could fall, and no one would ever find you.

And all of a sudden it was unbearable: the confined space; the darkness; the strange gloopy mud. Panic started to creep through her body, turning her palms sweaty, clutching at her throat. She felt as if the weight of rock above her was pressing down, squeezing the breath from her lungs. Katrina was desperate to get back into the open air.

"Dad! Dad! I don't like this. I've got to get out," Katrina bellowed at her father's rear end.

He was crawling up the tunnel ahead of her.

The need to escape was overwhelming. "I'm going back!" she called. There was no room to turn round, so she simply reversed – crawled backwards along the tunnel they had come down a few minutes before.

Or so she thought.

She only discovered her mistake when the ground below her suddenly gave way to the infinite space of what seemed like a bottomless chasm. Solid rock trickled away like sand through an egg timer. Katrina was suspended in the air for a split second, like a cartoon character who carries on running in mid-air. Then she fell.

But Katrina didn't fall down.

She fell up!

Katrina flew through the air and hit the cave's roof with a resounding *thwack*! The force of the impact dislodged her safety helmet, and before she could grab it, the helmet fell away below her. She looked down. Big mistake. Big, big mistake. The helmet was spinning into a black void, the light getting smaller and smaller and further and further away, until at last it disappeared altogether. There was no crash as it hit the floor of the cave. There seemed to be no floor for it to crash into. Katrina hadn't liked the confined space of the tunnel, but it was a million times worse hanging from a cave roof. Katrina – who hated heights more than any-thing else – was suspended over a bottomless black hole, with nothing holding her up but some weird sort of reverse gravity. She'd fallen up. Up??? *Up!!!!*

It was totally impossible. Wasn't it? But it all *felt* real enough.

Pressed against the rock, as if she was a fly that had been swatted onto the ceiling, Katrina lay dazed and blinking furiously.

"This is not good," she said to herself. "Dad!" she yelled desperately. Her voice echoed around the cave, but there was no answering call. She swallowed, took a deep breath and looked down again. The cave walls were glowing faintly, and as she got used to the dingy light she could see – at least fifty metres below her – the entrance to the tunnel that she had come through.

"WAAAAAAH! Get me out of here!" screamed a voice in her head.

"Stop it," she said firmly. "Stay calm. Now think, Katrina. What are you going to do?"

She looked at the cave roof.

"How on earth am I doing this?" she asked herself. "How am I sticking to the ceiling? Can I crawl? Can I move?"

Slowly, carefully, she pulled one hand off the rock. It came away with a slight sucking sound. She moved her hand a few inches and put it on the rock. It held. She moved a foot. It stuck back on in its new position.

OK, she thought, taking another deep breath. I'm upside down, but I can move across the ceiling if I want to. "*Do* I want to?" she asked herself. "Well I can't just hang around here for ever," she answered. "Better do something."

She started to crawl, edging forwards on her elbows towards the tunnel that led back to her dad. Something was pulling her onto the rock as strongly as if she was an iron filing on a huge magnet. Each move was a huge physical effort. At last she reached the place where the walls met the ceiling. She breathed a sigh of relief. If she could just slide down the wall she could find the tunnel that led back to Dad.

Katrina put her hand on the vertical surface, but it wouldn't stick. On the *side* walls she had no suction. She *couldn't* go back down. Katrina Picket was stranded on the ceiling.

An eerie calmness descended on her. The desperate icy tranquility of someone facing a most peculiar death. She was going to be on the ceiling until she starved. No one would ever find her. She laid her cheek gently against the rock and heaved a deep sigh.

Then she saw it.

About ten metres to her right, at the opposite

corner of the cave roof, was a heavy wooden door studded with bolts and with a huge iron ring for a handle. It looked like the entrance to a church.

A door in the roof of a cave? How peculiar. But what choice did she have?

"Better try it, I suppose," she said. Katrina crawled slowly and uncertainly towards the door, fingers and hands and knees working against the pull of the rock.

When she reached it, her fingers gave the iron ring an experimental prod. It was surprisingly warm, but otherwise seemed normal. Well, as normal as a door in the roof of a cave *can* seem. She grasped the iron ring firmly and turned it.

The door opened. Katrina lost suction. She swung through the air, and then Katrina was dangling by one hand over a void of infinite blackness.

"This can't get any worse," she squeaked.

But it did.

A snake appeared in the doorway. It was enormous. It was purple. Katrina was so shocked that she almost let go of the ring. The snake looked her straight in the eyes for a moment, then blinked and shook its head slightly, making a noise that

sounded very like an impatient *tut*. It slithered down her arm and wrapped itself around her waist, pulling her into a room.

Katrina didn't scream. She knew there was no point. She'd seen snakes eat things on the telly. If she expelled any breath, the snake would tighten its coils and she'd just die quicker.

Great, she thought despairingly as a single tear rolled down her cheek. Marvellous. Fantastic. I'm lunch. I'm going to be eaten by a purple cave snake. I've probably discovered a new species, and no one will ever know because I'll be *in* it... What a fantastic day out I'm having.

Katrina shut her eyes. She couldn't bear to look at the snake.

But then there was a small *pop!* and a smell of burnt-out fireworks and she realized the snake holding her had gone.

Katrina opened her eyes and flinched with shock. The snake had totally disappeared. But, standing by the wall of the circular room, watching her with intense interest, was an old man.

At least, she presumed it was a man. His hair was so long that it was hard to tell at first. It grew all the way to the floor, but stuck out as well, so that it surrounded him in a perfect circle. He looked like a human pompom.

Then he spoke.

"I'm ready," the man said eagerly. "Just show me the Danger, and I'll sort it out. Been dying to do something for centuries. Thought you would have needed me before now, actually, but better late than never, eh?"

"What?" said Katrina.

"Don't say 'what' say 'pardon'. Didn't your nurse teach you anything?"

"What?" she said again, and then corrected herself. "Pardon?"

He was gathering his hair up in handfuls, winding it into balls as if it was wool and then piling the hairballs on his head. When he had finished, he looked like he was wearing unusually large curlers.

"Must do something about this, the first chance I get," he said. "It's quite absurd, all this hair. I'll get a sword to it as soon as I've sorted out the Danger." He took his beard, rolled that up too and tied it in a very large knot under his chin.

"Now, young squire. Lead me to the Danger!"

"What danger?" said Katrina helplessly.

"*What* Danger?" he said. "*The* Danger! The Danger that brought you here... The Peril that threatens Albion! Lead me to it, and I'll see what I can do. I'm not promising anything. But prophesies are prophesies. I'll try my best."

Katrina blinked and scratched her nose. She wondered what Albion was, but didn't like to ask. This was all too weird for words. But he seemed like a nice sort of man, even if he was a bit strange, and she didn't want to be rude. She had been brought up to be polite, even if she did say "what" instead of "pardon".

"I'm very sorry," she said. "But I don't know what you're talking about."

The man sat down on a chair. "Squires these days," he complained. "Can't even carry a simple message without messing it up. Things aren't what they used to be. What's your name, boy?"

"Boy?" said Katrina indignantly. "I'm a girl, actually."

The man jumped in surprise. "A girl? A *girl*! A *female* squire? My, my, things *have* changed. What's your name?"

"Katrina Picket."

"Strange name," he said thoughtfully. "Well, Katrinapicket, take me to your knight and we'll sort everything out."

"Look, I'm really sorry, but I think you've got hold of the wrong end of the stick…"

"Stick?" The man looked confused. "I see no stick, young squire."

"No, no." Katrina tried to get back to the point. "Look, I'm not a squire, I don't know any knights, and no one *sent* me here. I got in by accident. I got lost in the tunnel – I was trying to get back out, actually. My dad will be really worried by now…"

"No one *sent* you?" The man was clearly puzzled.

"No."

"You got here by *accident*?"

"Yes."

He was perplexed, baffled. He rubbed his nose slowly with one finger, looking thoroughly confused. But then he slapped his hand against the wall. "I *refuse* to believe it!" he said decisively. "No, Katrinapicket, you did not wake me from my slumber by accident. A prophesy is a prophesy. I shall stay with you until all is made plain and the

Danger is revealed. Let us proceed!"

He looked at Katrina expectantly. Katrina looked helplessly back at him. The man seemed very determined. It was obviously pointless trying to explain anything to him.

"Lead the way!" he said enthusiastically, but with a note of impatience creeping into his voice.

Katrina was getting fed up. "I'm *lost*," she said irritably. "I don't *know* how to get out…"

"Oh, for heaven's sake!"

There was a small *pop!* and a whiff of fireworks. A large animal appeared where the strange man had been standing. It was purple and furry, with a pink snout and huge front paws. Digging paws.

"Stand back, Katrinapicket," it said.

Katrina obeyed. Now I'm taking orders from a giant purple mole, she thought. How much weirder is this day going to get?

The mole began to tunnel upwards with phenomenal speed. It pushed rocks and debris ahead of it, until it reached the surface. There was a distant *pop!* and Katrina saw sunlight way above her head and the old man peering down at her from the surface.

"Up you come then, Katrinapicket."

"How?" she bellowed. The walls of the tunnel the mole-man had dug were totally smooth and vertical. She couldn't possibly climb them.

There was a sparkle of purple light, and Katrina felt herself floating gently upwards, pirouetting in lazy circles until she reached daylight and fresh air. She landed very slowly on the soft grass in the glorious sunshine and sat with her eyes closed for a minute.

Then she felt a sharp prod in her ribs and the man was standing over her, saying impatiently, "Katrinapicket, take me to your knight."

"Katrina! Kat! Where are you?" Dad's desperate shouts were distant. He sounded like he was still underground, feverishly searching for the daughter he had somehow mislaid.

"Up here, Dad!" Katrina yelled as loudly as she could.

Dad emerged from a tunnel. He saw Katrina, sprinted across the grass and crushed her gratefully against his chest. "Thank heavens!" he gasped. "Why didn't you say you were coming

20

out? I've been frantic. I was about to call the rescue service!"

"Is this your knight, Katrinapicket?"

Dad released Katrina. He looked at the man. The man looked at Dad.

"Er… Katrina…?" said Dad.

"I met him underground," Katrina said matter-of-factly, as if it was perfectly normal to bump into strange old men while potholing. "He helped me out, actually. I got a bit lost."

Dad looked at the mountainous molehill that had not been there when he had parked the car that morning. He looked again at the man with the strange balls-of-wool hairstyle – it looked even more bizarre in the daylight than it had underground. Katrina noticed for the first time what the man was wearing – an extremely worn, extremely dirty, floor-length purple velvet dress.

Dad's eyes narrowed.

"And you would be…?" he asked.

The man looked at Dad. Raised his eyes skywards. "Oh, for heaven's sake! You, sir knight, are sadly lacking in your courtesies. You should kneel before me."

"Kneel?" said Dad, almost laughing. "Oh, really? And why might that be?"

The man was nettled. He drew himself up to his full height. Then he drew himself up some more. And more. He didn't stop. He grew taller and taller in front of their eyes. When he spoke, his voice echoed across the hills. "Because I can *obliterate* you with a *word*," the man boomed. "Because I can *destroy* your castle with a *look*. Because I can lay *waste* to your kingdom with a *blow* from my *fist*. *Kneel before me, for I am Merlin!*"

"Merlin?" said Dad in a high tight voice, looking up at the man who was now towering thirty feet tall, his hairballs as big as straw bales.

And Dad knelt. He really did. It wasn't as if he had much choice.

As soon as he had done it, Merlin shrunk to his usual size. "Thank heavens for that. So *exhausting*, these manifestations. Please don't make me do it again. Now, sir knight, what is your name?"

Dad was temporarily speechless, so Katrina said, "He's my dad."

"Strange name," Merlin said to himself. Then, "Sir Mydad, take me to your castle."

Danger?
What Danger?
(Friday afternoon)

Dangerous sports were one thing; supernatural manifestations were quite another as far as Dad was concerned. The first was something he understood and enjoyed, but when it came to the strange and unnatural growth of an elderly man in a purple dress, Dad's courage abandoned him. After Merlin's manifestation, Dad didn't say another word: he was in a state of shock.

Katrina was shocked too, but being of a more practical nature she was adjusting to the situation very quickly. After all, she reasoned, there were *loads* of things she didn't understand and couldn't explain: radio waves and silicon chips and digital technology. She just had to add a real live wizard to the list of inexplicable mysteries of the world.

All the way home, Dad drove very slowly and very carefully, with a lot more caution than usual. They inched their way slowly along the minor roads until they reached the main road, where Dad infuriated other motorists by steadfastly refusing to exceed 29 miles per hour, even where the speed limit was 60. Katrina knew exactly what he was up to. It was always Dad's solution to a domestic crisis – ignore the problem until it gives up and goes away. Dad seemed to think that if he concentrated hard enough on the road, the strange man in the back of the car would disappear.

Merlin didn't, of course. Merlin was going to stay until he had sorted out the Danger that was threatening Albion, whatever that was. Meanwhile, he was enjoying the novelty of being awake.

"My, my," he said. "How marvellous to see the sun again. What century did you say this was, young squire?"

24

"I didn't," answered Katrina. "But it's the twenty-first."

"Good heavens!" he exclaimed. "I have slept for nearly fifteen hundred years. Fancy that! And how things have changed!"

Merlin was delighted with the car. "Dear me!" he said. "How ingenious! Comfortable too. Glad to see horses have been replaced. Never could get the hang of the beasts myself. They bite with one end and make a terrible mess with the other... You could never go anywhere without getting a sore bottom. This is much nicer," he said, bouncing up and down on the back seat. "Glorious! Wonderful! Saw it all coming, of course."

"What do you mean?" asked Katrina.

"Can see the future, you know. One of my gifts. Can't imagine what they're teaching young squires these days," Merlin complained. "You ought to know *that*."

"Can you see what the danger is, then?" said Katrina.

"Ah ... well ... no, not exactly," Merlin confessed. "All a bit foggy at the moment. But things will be made plain, no doubt. Just give it time.

I shall give some thought to the matter when we arrive at the castle."

Merlin was astonished by the number of cars that flashed by as they drove along.

"Good heavens!" he said. "It's a different world. So many people! The kingdom must be very nearly full. I should never have recognized it..."

Just as well we're not on the motorway, thought Katrina. That would really freak him out.

"And where has the forest gone?" Merlin continued. "Where are the bears?"

"Erm..." Katrina looked at Dad for help – wildlife was more his sort of thing than hers – but he was looking straight ahead, pretending he was alone in the car.

"We don't have bears in England any more," she said. And to save time added, "Or wolves or lions or anything dangerous, really."

"What, no dragons?"

Katrina could see the colour drain from Dad's face, but he still didn't say anything.

"Definitely no dragons," she said firmly.

"Well, I say," Merlin was outraged. "That's taking things a little far. Ought to have left some room for dragons."

"Don't they eat people?" Katrina asked.

"Only on Wednesdays," said Merlin indignantly. "Jolly useful things, dragons. You should have left some room for them. That was badly done, Katrinapicket." Merlin huffed crossly. He sank into a sulk for the rest of the journey.

As they approached Bristol, they passed a large mansion set in acres of parkland.

Merlin peered through the trees at it. "Is that your castle? A little on the small side, perhaps, but it will suffice."

"No," said Katrina. "It's not. And we don't actually live in a castle. People don't any more. We live in a house. It's very small, really. Are you sure you want to stay?"

"Quite sure," said Merlin, although he sounded disappointed. "A prophesy is a prophesy, and must be obeyed."

What on earth is Mum going to say? thought Katrina.

Dad pulled up outside their house. He turned off the engine, got out of the car, went straight round to the back and locked himself in the garden shed without saying a word.

Katrina could see that she was just going to have to manage alone.

She helped Merlin out of the car. He seemed to have a problem working out where to put his feet in a confined space, and one of his hairballs had become unwound and was tangled in the seat belt.

"Come and meet my mum," she said, when she had freed him. She led Merlin up the path and into the house.

Mum was very calm about it all. She didn't scream or faint. She didn't do any of the things Katrina had thought she might when she walked in with a total stranger and said, "This is Merlin. He's come to stay for a bit."

Mum simply looked up from the book she was reading and said dreamily – as if her mind was still trapped between the covers – "Merlin? Oh, dear. Is Albion in peril, then?"

"Indeed it is, Lady Mymum," Merlin answered.

"Better take him up to the spare room, Katrina," she said calmly. "The bed's made up."

Katrina led Merlin upstairs. Of course, Mum was used to having weird and wonderful theatrical types dropping in with no warning. Adrian, Katrina's brother, was a lighting technician for the Normal Theatre Company. They specialized in large outdoor events – festivals, carnivals, that kind of thing. They were touring in Australia at the moment. Sometimes Mum was called on to provide a room for visiting actors when they had a special event on. She kept the spare room ready just in case.

It was small – barely wide enough to accommodate the single bed and the chest of drawers with the tiny television perched perilously on top. The pink wallpaper had circus horses dancing all over it.

Merlin shuddered when he saw it. "Horses," he said in disgust. "No, no." He waved his hand. There was a faint *pop!* and the horses changed to dragons. A faint whiff of burnt-out fireworks circled the room

"Much better," he said. He looked under the bed. "Katrinapicket," Merlin said with a frown. "Where is my chamber pot?"

Katrina looked blank.

"I need to relieve myself," he explained. "There is no chamber pot under the bed. Please bring me one. It's been nearly fifteen hundred years – I am very uncomfortable."

"Erm…" Katrina blushed. "We don't do it like that any more." She led him to the bathroom and pointed to the toilet. "You have to do it in there."

"In there…?" Merlin looked uncertain.

"Yes, and then you flush it." She demonstrated the flush.

Merlin jumped.

"Good heavens! Does it do that every time?"

"Oh yes…"

Katrina turned her back quickly. Merlin was hitching up his dress. She sidled out of the bathroom and waited for a very long time on the landing. At last Merlin came out, and she followed him back to the spare room.

"Do you need anything?" she asked. "Food? Or a cup of tea or anything?"

"No, Katrinapicket. You may go now. I shall give some thought to the Danger. Let me have peace while I envision the Peril that threatens Albion."

He sat cross-legged on the bed. His eyes rolled back into his head, and he started to hum.

Katrina went back downstairs. Mum was still sitting at the kitchen table, sipping tea and reading a book about gardening.

Katrina sat down beside her. "How do you know about Albion being in peril?" she asked.

"Mmmmm?" said Mum vaguely. She was deep in herbaceous perennials.

"You said something about Albion," persisted Katrina. "What is Albion, anyway?"

Mum looked up. "Albion? It's the old name for England. Don't you know the legend?"

"No."

"Oh. I suppose the Normal Theatre lot are going to do something on it when they get back from Australia. Well, according to the story Merlin is asleep, sealed in a cave, but he will wake when Albion's in peril."

"And he's awake now…" said Katrina thoughtfully.

"Oh, ha, ha. Very funny," was Mum's only response. "Arranged it with Adrian, did you, before he left?" She didn't wait for Katrina to answer. "I don't know what Adrian expects us to do with him. He's going to have to amuse himself. I won't have time to look after him."

"I'll do it," said Katrina quickly. "I could show him round a bit. You know, do some touristy stuff."

"*Could you*? That would be nice." Mum returned to her book.

"When was Merlin last awake then?" Katrina wondered aloud. "I mean, what was it like back then?"

Mum laughed. "Why don't you ask Merlin? I'm sure he'll be happy to fill you in."

"I can't," Katrina answered. "He's gone into a trance thing."

"These theatrical types!" Mum tutted without looking up. "Meditation and yoga and Lord knows what. Always doing something strange, aren't they? Preparing for his role, I suppose. He must be one of those method actors. You know, the ones who have to really *live* the part. They go round all day pretending to be Hamlet or Lady Macbeth. Daft lot."

"Where did Merlin live?" Katrina asked. "Do you know?"

Mum closed her book with a sigh. She didn't like being interrupted when she was reading, but she could see Katrina wasn't going to leave the subject alone. "He's part of all those old Round Table legends. You must have heard of them: King Arthur, Queen Guinevere, knights in shining armour, Lancelot... All that sort of stuff. I read a book about it once. Merlin was the wizard at King Arthur's court. Camelot, it was called. And everything was perfect until an evil knight started to destroy it all. Mordred, I think his name was. Nasty piece of work. Anyway, it all ended in disaster. There was a huge battle. It was an absolute bloodbath. Everyone killed everyone else. Arthur's body was taken off to the island of Avalon, and Guinevere went off to be a nun. End of story. OK?"

Mum opened her book again and was soon lost amongst drifts of cornflowers.

The conversation was over. Katrina knew that she wouldn't get any more information out of Mum that day, so she wandered into the front room and switched on the television.

The news was on. She watched for stories of danger and peril. The news was full of them. Riots,

34

protests, wars: there were terrible things happening all over the world, but no *new* disaster as far as Katrina could make out. Nothing that threatened England's actual existence...

The local news started. There was a bit about the preparations for the royal visit in two days' time. The Queen was coming to open a new art gallery in the centre of Bristol.

Then suddenly, in glorious Technicolor, there was a picture of the mountainous molehill that Merlin had created. Katrina switched off quickly. She didn't want Mum to overhear that bit. Mum might realize that Merlin had something to do with it, and then she'd work out that Merlin wasn't an eccentric actor at all. Mum would refuse to have him in the house. She'd force him to leave somehow. And Katrina had the uneasy feeling that something important had started to happen. She didn't want Merlin to go.

She wasn't sure why not. It could have been simple curiosity, pure nosiness – she was burning to know why he had woken – but there was something else too... She felt ... what? Katrina felt ... *responsible*.

At teatime, Dad claimed to be busy and refused to come out of the shed. Mum pushed a cheese sandwich under the door for him. Then Mum and Katrina ate in the kitchen while Mum carried on leafing through her book.

"I quite fancy doing a Japanese garden this summer," mused Mum. "A total makeover. Bamboo and water and pebbles and things. Sort of poised and tranquil. What do you think, Katrina?"

"Mmmm," answered Katrina. "Sounds great." But she wasn't really listening. Katrina had her mind on other things.

Merlin didn't come downstairs all evening. When Katrina went to bed, she peeped round the door, just to check on him.

He was still sitting cross-legged on the bed, but now he was murmuring to himself, "Danger, the Danger," over and over again. His voice was low and hollow. It was a bit spooky.

Katrina shivered and closed the door quickly.

The murmuring went on all night.

The Danger is Revealed

(Saturday)

They were all tired and bleary-eyed in the morning.

Mum was cross. "I'm going to have to have a word with Adrian about this one as soon as he gets home," she said. "He can't stay if he's going to do that all night."

"Katrina will have a word with Merlin," Dad said pointedly. "Won't you, Kat?"

She nodded. She was pleased to hear Dad speaking again. He had been in the shed so long yesterday that Katrina had wondered if he'd ever come out again. Dad obviously wanted to go on letting Mum believe Merlin was an eccentric actor for as long as possible. Katrina silently agreed. They exchanged significant looks, and then Dad swallowed the rest of his toast and hurriedly left for work.

Merlin came down about ten minutes later, looking very puzzled. His hairballs were flattened and his face was forlorn. "All night, Katrinapicket," he sighed sadly. "All night I searched my inner eye, but I can see nothing. I find no Danger."

"Well, that's good, isn't it?" said Katrina.

"No, it is *not* good," he replied, slapping his hand down on the table with such force that the orange juice carton jumped a centimetre in the air. "You did not wake me for nothing. There *is* a Danger. *Somewhere*. But how on earth to find it? That's the question... I confess I am a little perplexed."

Merlin sat down heavily. A hairball unravelled and plopped into Katrina's cornflakes.

"Bad hair day?" Mum asked him.

"Oh, Lady Mymum," he said pitifully. "A bad hair day indeed." He retrieved his hairball and peered into Katrina's bowl. "What strange food-stuff is that?" he asked her.

"Cornflakes," said Katrina. She'd suddenly gone off them.

"I expect you'd like a full English, wouldn't you?" said Mum, putting a steaming plate of bacon, sausages and eggs in front of Merlin. "It's what the Normal Theatre lot usually want. And you must be hungry after all this time." She laughed, and started to load the dishwasher.

Katrina was glad that Mum's back was turned. She didn't think Mum would take too kindly to Merlin picking up a fried egg with his fingers.

"Use a knife and fork," she hissed. "Like this." She seized Merlin's cutlery and gave a quick demonstration, cutting Merlin's sausage into bite-sized pieces, as if he were a toddler.

Merlin studied the fork with deep suspicion. Then, with intense concentration, he grasped his cutlery and started to eat. It was a slow task, fraught with anxiety and tension. Crispy bacon kept pinging in different directions. And the fried egg seemed to have a life of its own – skidding around the plate every time Merlin tried to spear it, and sliding off the fork when he attempted to transport it into his mouth. But eventually his plate was cleared, and Katrina – who had scraped the remains of her cornflakes into the bin – grilled them both a slice of toast.

Merlin nibbled it carefully. He was delighted with the marmalade. "What an exotic confection!" he exclaimed. "Magnificent! Marvellous!"

But once he'd finished his last mouthful, Merlin's brow furrowed and his face resumed its worried expression. He pushed back his chair, heaved a very deep sigh and said, "Lady Mymum... May I borrow Sir Mydad's sword?"

"Pardon?" said Mum.

"His sword," said Merlin, beginning to unwind a hairball. "If I could borrow his sword, I could hack the whole lot off."

"That would be a shame," said Mum. "You'd spoil your look."

"It may be part of the problem," Merlin continued, regardless. "Too much weight on my head... Perhaps that's why my inner eye has failed."

"I know exactly what you mean," said Mum sympathetically. "It's terribly difficult to think straight when your hair needs doing, isn't it? Tell you what, there's a hairdresser on the corner. Why don't you take him up there, Katrina? See if they can do anything for him. Don't let them take too much off, though – I don't think the Normal Theatre lot would be too pleased if their Merlin came into rehearsals with a skinhead. We'd be in all sorts of trouble then." She laughed at her own joke, and failed to see Merlin's baffled expression.

The hairdresser had never seen anything like it.

"Wow, this is *amazing*! *Wow*. How long did it take you to grow it?"

"A few hundred years," said Merlin irritably. "If only someone would bring me a sword, I could just cut it off."

The hairdresser was giggling. "A few hundred years! He's funny, innee, your friend." She fetched a wide-toothed comb and attempted to rake it through his hair. "You've let it get ever so out of condition, though," she said, tutting noisily. "Terrible split ends too. Tell you what – I'll get the worst of it off, then we'll wash and style it. How's that?"

Merlin looked at Katrina. She nodded at him.

"Very well," he said reluctantly.

The hairdresser started slicing through Merlin's hair at about shoulder level, and trimmed most of his beard off too. "Look at that lot!" she said.

"Enough to stuff a jolly good mattress," said Merlin.

The hairdresser giggled. She led him to the sink, sat him down and started showering his head.

"Oh!" said Merlin with surprise. "Good heavens!" The shock of a jet of warm water hitting his head for the first time in centuries (and perhaps for the first time ever) quite unsettled him. But then Merlin started to enjoy himself. "What an extraordinary sensation! Quite remarkable. Terribly refreshing."

Then the hairdresser sat him in front of the mirror, and said, "Now, Mr Merlin, we want to go for the windswept look, I think. As if you've just come in from a long walk. We don't want anything too neat, do we?" She snipped and trimmed, and finally blow-dried it, and in the end, Merlin looked as if he had walked out of a shampoo commercial.

"That feels much better, Katrinapicket," he said.

"Now perhaps I'll be able to think more clearly."

Katrina hoped it would work. It had cost her all the pocket money she had been saving for the holidays.

When they got back home, Mum was drinking coffee in the kitchen and was clearly in a chatty mood.

"Your hair looks marvellous," she said, holding out a mug of coffee to Merlin.

He sniffed it suspiciously, prodding an exploratory finger into the dark brown liquid and licking it, before taking the mug from her.

"So … Merlin," said Mum, winking at Katrina. "How are you coping? Things must have changed a bit since you were last awake."

"Oh, indeed, Lady Mymum. And not all for the better. Albion is sadly lacking in dragons. It was a mistake, I think, not leaving sufficient room for them."

"I don't think people liked being eaten," said Mum.

Merlin sniffed. "But it was only on *Wednesdays*."

Mum tactfully changed the subject. "So, what's

Morgan Le Fay up to these days?" She looked at Katrina and explained, "She was King Arthur's half-sister. A real baddie."

"She is Everywhere and Nowhere," intoned Merlin mysteriously. "She did not fall asleep, as I did. She remained in the world. She is the evil that dwells in men's hearts…"

"That explains a lot," sniffed Mum.

"But I do not sense her presence now," Merlin continued thoughtfully. "No … she is not involved—"

"So why wake up now?" Mum interrupted Merlin. "You missed some good things last century. We could have done with you in the Second World War, you know – England was in terrible peril then."

"Wars," Merlin said dismissively. "Can't be doing with wars. Leave them to you lot to sort out. You start them – you can jolly well finish them. That's why I left Arthur in the end, you know. Could see that final battle coming a long way off."

"Merlin foretold it," Mum said to Katrina. "He warned Arthur what was coming, but it didn't make any difference."

"Leave them to it, that's what I say. Human

nature, you know. Not much I can do about that. Decided I just had to let things run their course. That's why I went off."

"Oh, really?" said Mum, a teasing twinkle in her eye. "And what about Nimue?"

Merlin flushed a pretty shade of pink. He coughed and rubbed his nose. "Harmless little infatuation, Lady Mymum. It was a very long time ago. Not very courteous of you to bring it up." He looked a little peeved.

"What's Nimue?" asked Katrina.

"Not what – who," said Mum. "She was a lady of the lake. Merlin fell in love with her. She got him to teach her everything he knew about magic, and then she cast a spell to put him to sleep. She was the one who sealed him in the cave."

"She most certainly did not!" Merlin was furious. He leapt out of his chair, knocking the table and upsetting his half-finished cup of coffee.

Katrina mopped up while Merlin continued to grumble.

"*Typical*," he complained, pacing up and down the kitchen, completely oblivious to the domestic mayhem he had caused. "Go to sleep for a few hundred years, and people start telling all sorts of stories about you. None of them true. Put *myself* to sleep, I did."

Katrina finished mopping up. She pushed his chair back towards the table and Merlin sat down without a glance in her direction.

"Could *see* what was going to happen, you know," he mumbled. "Arthur in love with Guinevere, Guinevere in love with Lancelot and that ghastly little Mordred running around trying to spoil things for everyone. Stirring up trouble. Sowing discord. Setting everyone at each other's throats. No way of preventing it. Could see it would all end in tears. Couldn't bear to watch. Sent *myself* to sleep."

Merlin paused to look for his coffee, found the empty mug, and stared into it with a puzzled expression on his face. "Hmmm," he grunted. Then he changed the subject. "Prophesied I'd come back, you know. Promised to wake up if Albion was in mortal peril. And here I am!" he finished, banging the table triumphantly.

There was a long, uncomfortable pause.

"But where's the peril?" Mum's question

dropped into the kitchen like a lead weight.

"Ah..." Merlin was instantly deflated. He stroked his neatly trimmed beard and heaved a tragically deep sigh. "Yes ... there does seem to be a problem with the Peril. I have searched and searched my inner eye and cannot find where on earth the Danger lies."

Mum finished her coffee, picked up her gardening gloves and opened the back door. She gave Katrina another tremendous wink. As she went out into the garden, Mum called back over her shoulder, "Then perhaps you should try the heavens."

Which is why Merlin spent his second night at Katrina's house lying in the garden, staring at the sky, murmuring, "The Danger. Show me the Danger."

"Lord knows what the neighbours think," complained Mum. "He's worse than Yang Chan."

Yang Chan was a Chinese acrobat who had stayed with them the year before. He had got up very early every morning to do his t'ai chi exercises. Fences meant nothing to him. Mum had looked out one morning and, to her horror, had seen him standing on one leg in a trance on the neighbours' patio.

Katrina didn't think the neighbours would object to Merlin. They put up with the family with no complaints. There was Mum redoing the garden every couple of years, or embarking on some new interior design scheme that involved endless banging and crashing. Then there were Adrian's occasional experiments with lighting effects. One time he'd tried illuminating the clouds with a strobe light, and most of Bristol had thought the Martians were coming. The army had nearly been called out. And there had been the time when Dad had decided to test some of his rock climbing gear by abseiling out of the bedroom windows.

At least Merlin was quiet. They would hardly know he was there.

When Katrina looked out of her bedroom window later, she couldn't even see Merlin in the dark. It was odd, though, because she could feel his presence. She knew he hadn't moved an inch. And even though Merlin was muttering too quietly to be heard indoors, his words had got inside her head somehow. "The Danger. Show me the Danger." They were beating out a rhythm inside her brain. Katrina fell into an uneasy doze, a feeling of vague menace hovering around her like a cloud of buzzing insects.

At 4 a.m. there was a wild shout from the garden.

Merlin bounded up the stairs, threw open the door of Katrina's bedroom and shouted, "Katrinapicket, I have found it!"

He pointed out of her window at the night sky. "It's there!" he said, his finger trembling with excitement. "It's coming from there. And if I can't find a means to vanquish it, it will destroy all Albion!"

A Royal Visit
(Sunday morning)

Suddenly Katrina was as fully awake as if Merlin had doused her with a bucket of iced water. Her eyes followed Merlin's pointing finger.

"What is it?" she whispered faintly. "*What*'s coming?"

"A fireball," answered Merlin grimly. "A monstrous rock plucked from the heavens themselves. It hurtles towards Albion even as we speak."

Katrina was very glad she was still in bed. She wasn't prone to fainting, but just at that moment she thought she might have passed out with sheer terror if she hadn't already been lying down.

"When?" she squeaked. "How long until it gets here?"

Merlin squinted at the night sky. Then he tutted in irritation. "I cannot say for certain," he said crossly, pointing an accusing finger at the street-lights. "These ludicrous orange torches cloud my inner eye. I cannot see the heavens clearly... But I think ... no, I *feel*, it is but days away, young squire. Four ... perhaps five... There is no time to waste. Up you get, Katrinapicket." Merlin pulled her from her bed. "We need to see the King at once."

"But it's the middle of the night," Katrina said.

"The Danger is approaching, young squire," Merlin said sternly. "We cannot lie in bed while Albion is in peril."

"I know *that*," said Katrina. No one was going to accuse *her* of ignoring the Danger. "I just wondered where we're going?"

"To the King! To Camelot!"

"Ah..." Katrina sat back down on her bed. "It's not there any more. Camelot, I mean. And it's not a king – it's a queen."

"A queen? A *queen*? Good heavens!" Merlin took a moment to recover from the shock. "Well, we must get to Her Majesty in all haste and alert her to the Peril."

"No, no, no," said Katrina. "It doesn't work like that. You can't just walk in and see her."

"But we're her *subjects*," said Merlin indignantly. "A queen ought to see her *subjects*. We must go and seek an audience."

Katrina was confused. "An *audience*?" she repeated. "What do you want an audience for?"

"An audience … an interview … a discussion. Call it what you will – I must speak with the monarch straight away. Come on, Katrinapicket!" He tugged her arm impatiently.

"But you can't just go and speak to her," Katrina protested. "She's got guards and things to stop people getting in."

"Does she *never* speak to her people?" Merlin enquired.

"Well, she does, yes." Katrina racked her brains. "Sometimes she does walkabouts and things. You can talk to her then if you're lucky." Inspiration lit up Katrina's face. She clapped her hand to her forehead. "She's coming *here*! To Bristol – it said so on the news the other night. I think it's today. She's opening the new art gallery. We can try to see her then if you like…" Then a thought struck her. "Why do you need to see her anyway?"

"It's the way things are," said Merlin briskly. "I need the consent of the monarch to rescue Albion from the Peril. Can't do any magic otherwise – not in the service of Albion, anyway. It's strictly by permission, you know. Got to have the Royal Assent."

"Gosh," said Katrina. "I had no idea it was so complicated."

"Can't think what they're teaching squires these days," grumbled Merlin. "Katrinapicket, you are woefully ignorant."

"Sorry," she said, humbly.

However impatient they both were for action, neither of them could do anything until the Queen arrived. Katrina lay in bed, thinking things over, but at last she managed to get back to sleep.

Merlin, however, wandered down to the kitchen and searched the cupboards until he found what he wanted. Then he tramped back upstairs and sat on his bed in the spare room, absent-mindedly eating marmalade straight from the jar with a fork. The stars were beginning to fade now as the sun neared the horizon. Merlin stared up at them. He looked into the future. And wherever his inner eye focussed, he saw flames and destruction: he saw the annihilation of Albion.

By 11 a.m. Katrina and Merlin stood pressed against a barrier with a crowd of excited onlookers, waiting for the arrival of the royal cavalcade.

The new art gallery was a splendid modern building, standing in the middle of Bristol's redeveloped waterfront. It was a cube of concrete and glass that reflected the summer sky: clouds scudded across its surface. An extraordinary fountain ran the entire length of the building. Water didn't jet and spurt – it glided and slid over steel and slate.

"Nice, isn't it?" said Katrina.

Merlin merely sniffed. "Useless," he remarked. "Utterly useless. No towers, no turrets. How would one repel invaders?" He pointed at the fountain. "That moat would scarce deter a slug." Then he waved a hand at something Katrina hadn't noticed. "The dragon's the best bit."

To the right of the art gallery, tucked round the side between the building and the road, stood a very large statue of a dragon. It was on its hind legs, wings outstretched, mouth slightly open. It had been garishly and very badly painted in purple and green – as if someone had slapped it on with a trowel. It was hideous.

"That's more like it," Merlin was saying with approval. "I used to know a dragon. Good friend, he was. Name of Desmond. Fond of chess."

Policemen with fierce looking alsatians were walking up and down the street. One dog sniffed Merlin and then tried to lick his slippered feet.

"Be gone, wolf," Merlin muttered under his breath.

There was a sparkle of purple light, and the dog backed away. The policeman with him looked at Merlin through narrowed eyes, but Katrina smiled up at him innocently, and eventually he moved on.

At 12 noon precisely, three enormous black cars drew up and several men in black who must have been bodyguards stepped out. A moment later, the

Queen followed. She was dressed in a pale green dress, with matching hat, coat and handbag. Even though Katrina had never met her in real life, the Queen was familiar and unmistakeable to her, but Merlin didn't react. He continued to stare at the cars expectantly.

"Where is she?" he asked Katrina.

"That's her," Katrina said, pointing. "The one in green."

Merlin was shocked. "*That* is the monarch?"

"Yes..."

"*She* is the fairest lady in all Albion?"

"Well, no..."

"She is not the true queen," said Merlin decisively, and tried to walk away. But the crowd was packed so tightly that he couldn't move.

"It *is* the Queen, honestly Merlin. She's coming closer – don't you want to speak to her? Come on! You said you had to get the Royal Assent!"

"No dragons, and now an old *crone* for a queen," Merlin grumbled. "Beginning to wish I'd never woken."

The Queen approached them. She chatted about the weather to the flag-waving crowd. Katrina and

Merlin waited anxiously for her to reach them, but she got within two feet of Merlin and then crossed the road to talk to some people on the other side.

"Oh, no!" sighed Katrina. "We'll have to attract her attention. I know, I need a bunch of flowers – she always accepts flowers – let's go and get some, quick!"

There was a shower of purple sparks, a waft of burnt-out fireworks, and Katrina found herself holding a bunch of green leaves. Merlin had disappeared.

"Ow!" she squealed, and dropped them. They weren't quite what she had had in mind.

There was a *pop!* and Merlin was back.

"I wanted something pretty," Katrina hissed at him. "Not a bunch of stinging nettles!"

"Useful things, nettles," said Merlin huffily. "Thought she might want some nice soup."

"Try something different," said Katrina. "Hurry up, she's coming this way."

Pop! This time when Merlin transformed, Katrina found herself holding a bunch of enormous purple snapdragons. Their scent was curious – strongly floral, with a faint but familiar whiff of

58

fireworks. They were ten times the size of the ones that Mum had once grown in the garden. It worked – the Queen looked their way.

Girl.

Bunch of flowers.

It had the same effect on the Queen as an aniseed trail on a bloodhound. She crossed the street again and said, "Ixtraordinirry flaars."

"Pardon?" said Katrina. It took a moment for her to adjust to the Queen's accent.

"Ixtraordinirry flaars," the Queen repeated.

"Oh... Extraordinary flowers!" said Katrina, translating for the Merlin-bunch-of-snapdragons.

"Nivver sin inything quaite laike thim bifore... Did yew grow thim yoursilf?"

"Erm ... well ... kind of..." stuttered Katrina.

"Charming. Quaite, quaite charming. Will dun."

The Queen reached out to take the flowers. Katrina held on. There was a slight tussle.

Then, the snapdragons spoke.

"Your Majesty, I have grave news," they said.

The Queen looked at the flowers. She looked at Katrina. Katrina smiled a wobbly smile.

"Albion is in peril," continued the snapdragons.

"Oh, rilly?" said the Queen, looking at Katrina. "And what piril maight thit be?"

"It will come from the heavens," said the snapdragons.

"From the hivins?" said the Queen politely.

"Grant the Royal Assent so that I may use my magic to defend Albion," the snapdragons pleaded.

"What an ixtraordinirry tilent yew hiv," said the Queen to Katrina. "Hiy lorng hiv yew bin a vintriloquist?"

"I..." said Katrina. "Um ... well ... I ... don't know..." she tailed off helplessly.

"Give me the Royal Assent," demanded the snapdragons.

"Virry imusing," said the Queen, but she looked a little irritated. "Kirry orn." She turned to go.

"*Give me the Royal Assent!*" yelled the snapdragons at the Queen's retreating back.

But it was no good – she had gone.

"Leave her alone," said the man standing next to Katrina. "Poor lady, she's doing her best. Stop making fun of her."

"I wasn't," said Katrina. "We just wanted to talk to her."

The man looked hard at Katrina, then muttered under his breath, "Blooming nutters."

"Let's go home," Katrina said to the snapdragons.

When they arrived home, it was clear that Mum had spent most of the day visiting garden centres. Brochures littered the kitchen table.

"I can't decide," said Mum, as soon as Katrina and Merlin walked in. "Should I go for Mount Fuji or Last Emperor?"

They appeared to be types of pebble.

"It hardly matters, Lady Mymum," said Merlin bitterly, and he stumped up the stairs without saying another word. The bed creaked loudly as Merlin crashed despairingly down onto it.

"Not *another* bad hair day," tutted Mum. "He's a bit moody, isn't he? Can't imagine why the Normal Theatre lot employed him. They usually send us quite cheery types."

"Oh … well…" muttered Katrina. "There's some sort of … erm … technical problem that's bothering him. You know the sort of thing… I'll take him up a cup of tea."

She would have taken him some toast and marmalade, too, but she couldn't seem to find the jar.

Merlin's gloom was so thick that Katrina could almost see it seeping under the bedroom door.

When she went in, Merlin turned his troubled face towards her. "The Danger draws closer, Katrinapicket," he said quietly. "I feel it growing stronger every moment. And I didn't get the Royal Assent! Without it I can do no magic! I can do nothing! Nothing! Albion shall surely perish!"

Katrina set down his tea on top of the chest of drawers. "I don't understand," she said. "You can do transformations. Don't they count as magic?"

"That's only Minor Magic," sniffed Merlin.

"But you're a wizard," said Katrina. "Why do you need permission?"

"Sorcerer, if you don't mind," said Merlin huffily. "Let me explain, young squire. To protect Albion one must have authority from the monarch – the rightful king. In my day it was King Arthur. He protected Albion, you see. He was its guardian; he held the kingdom in his care. I could do nothing without his permission. To be a monarch is a sacred duty. The king is bound to his kingdom –

enmeshed with it. It has its own powerful magic, Katrinapicket. One cannot break its laws safely."

Merlin sighed hopelessly and held his head in his hands.

"There must be *something* we can do," said Katrina desperately. "Isn't there *anyone* who can help?"

Suddenly Merlin sat up. The light of an idea was shining in his eyes.

"You are quite right, Katrinapicket," he said with grim determination. "It is time to wake King Arthur."

Raising Avalon
(Sunday afternoon)

Merlin was striding back towards the water-front with Katrina jogging along breathlessly at his heels.

"We need a lake," said Merlin, as Katrina grabbed hold of his velvet dress to prevent him from walking into the stream of traffic. "Somewhere quiet. Clear, deep water. The bigger the better. Where's the nearest one?"

Katrina steered him towards a pedestrian crossing. She thought hard. "Chew Valley, I suppose," she said. "Or Blagdon."

"Then let us proceed forthwith."

"No," said Katrina. "We can't walk – it's miles away. We'd have to go in the car, or catch a bus or something."

"No time," said Merlin.

They were halfway across a footbridge that spanned the docks. Merlin stopped suddenly. "We'll just have to do it here."

"Here! In the docks!" Katrina was horrified. "What are you going to do?"

"We," said Merlin simply, "are going to wake Arthur."

"But…" Katrina stuttered helplessly. "People will notice, won't they?" Somehow she didn't think Merlin *should* be doing magic. Not in broad day-light. Not without the Royal Assent.

"Sadly, yes. People will notice, without a doubt. But it can't be helped. I had hoped to be more dis-creet, but the matter is urgent. And it *is* in the service of Albion," Merlin said. "Let us summon Avalon!"

"Avalon?" gasped Katrina. Her mind raced. She'd heard of Avalon. Mum had said something about it. "Isn't that an island?"

"Indeed. It is the isle where Arthur sleeps."

"You mean it's *here*? In Bristol? In the *docks*?"

"Avalon is Everywhere and Nowhere," intoned Merlin mysteriously.

"Oh … *right*," sniffed Katrina, rolling her eyes skywards. "One of *those*."

Merlin sighed. "How can I explain, Katrinapicket? Avalon is in another dimension. It is not part of this world, but we can make it so. We must bring it into being with an invocation."

"That sounds like pretty major magic to me," said Katrina suspiciously.

Merlin scratched his nose. He looked distinctly shifty. "Well, not *technically* speaking…" he said. "Not if *you* do it."

"Me?"

"Yes, Katrinapicket … *you*."

Merlin rolled up his sleeves. "You're merely a squire, you see. You *are* under twelve?"

Katrina nodded.

Merlin grunted his approval. "Below the age of magical responsibility! Not answerable for your actions. You can wriggle around the rules a bit, and no one will even notice. Not if we're lucky. And if necessary, it can be explained away as a juvenile prank, a kind of supernatural accident. You see?"

Katrina didn't see. She didn't see at all. And who made the rules anyway? She was way out of her depth. But it was exciting. Exciting and a bit terrifying.

And she had to do it.

The thought dropped into her head like a pebble into a pool.

She *had* to raise Avalon.

Merlin gave his instructions, whispering them quietly into her ear.

"Is that it?" asked Katrina. "Don't I have to wave a wand or anything?"

Merlin sniffed. "Wands are for amateurs," he said dismissively. "No, Katrinapicket. Just say the words with enough conviction and Avalon will appear. Fix your eyes on the middle of the water – just where that seagull is. Now imagine an island you have seen before – that will help with the materialization. Concentrate very hard, young squire. Let's see what you can do."

Katrina didn't think for a minute that she would

be able to do it. But then she had never dreamt that she could hang from a cave roof either, so she was obviously capable of more than she knew. Anyway, she had to try. The fate of Albion depended on it. She closed her eyes and thought of an island – the one she had seen on holiday in Scotland the summer before. It was small – no more than fifteen metres or so across – and had a Rapunzel-like stone tower standing in the middle. Dad had rowed them out to it so they could picnic on its beach. She recalled the grey shingle, the tough grass beyond, the sound of the loch lapping against the shore, the smell and the colour of the place, the cloud of buzzing, biting flies that had nearly driven them mad… Maybe she could do without the insects. She wiped them from her mind and started again. When finally she had the picture clearly in her head she opened her eyes, fixed them on the seagull and spoke the words that Merlin had whispered in her ear:

> *"Earth, air, fire, water,*
> *Elements flow free.*
> *Bring dreamers to this solid world,*
> *Draw Avalon to thee."*

Nothing happened.

Nothing.

Not a ripple; not a splash. Nothing changed. The seagull bobbed on the olive-green water, completely undisturbed.

Tears of disappointment and frustration pricked the back of Katrina's eyes. She swallowed hard. Merlin rested his hand on her shoulder – a comforting gesture that completely failed to comfort her. It hadn't worked. She'd blown it. Albion was doomed.

Merlin opened his mouth to speak. But at that moment there was a faint bubbling noise – like the sound of a distant kettle coming to the boil.

Then the water in the dock started to steam and froth. The seagull flew up with a startled screech. And the water parted, separating in the middle of the docks like a pair of curtains being opened.

A single stone appeared first, rising up, spiralling, corkscrewing slowly out of the water. It was the top of the tower.

It emerged exactly as Katrina had pictured it – inch by inch, stone by stone, blade of grass by blade of grass – a perfect replica of the one in the

Scottish loch. *With* the shingle beach and *without* the midges.

Katrina's mouth fell open.

It was just as well she had imagined a small island. By the time it had fully risen, it filled the harbour and was wedged firmly between the dock walls.

Before Katrina had time to admire it, the mist swirled again. It got denser. Then formed itself into a point and was sucked in through the arched doorway of the tower. The mist formed a round tube shape like a tunnel that seemed to lead from Bristol into another world. Katrina squinted into the mist. A shape was visible. A figure on horseback, approaching rapidly from a long way off. As the rider drew nearer, Katrina could see it was a knight. A knight in shining armour. A real one.

He was very tall. He ducked his head as he rode out of the tower. Then he rode over the island, across its shingle beach and onto the dockside. The sound of his horse's hooves rang out as they struck the paving stones.

"Arthur!" Merlin's voice was no more than a raw whisper, heavy with emotion. "Arthur!"

Arthur leant down from his horse and clutched Merlin's hand. "Merlin! Well met, my friend."

They looked at each other. All that Arthur had seen and suffered since Merlin had sealed himself within the cave was in that look. And Merlin's knowledge of it. His sadness. His understanding. Katrina could see that they were both deeply moved. She felt a lump rise in her throat.

There was a weighty pause. Then, "There is work to be done?" asked Arthur in his deep warm voice.

"Albion needs its true king," Merlin answered crisply. "You must ride again and claim the crown."

"Oh," said Katrina. She didn't like the sound of that. Arthur looked at her for the first time. Her heart missed a beat. He had black curly hair and deep brown eyes. He was very handsome, but even more appealing was the air of absolute goodness that encircled him. Katrina felt that he could be trusted. Absolutely and totally. Whatever happened, you would feel safe if Arthur was there. Kindness oozed out of every pore. How on earth could Guinevere love anyone else? thought Katrina.

The mist swirled again.

"Hang on," said Katrina indignantly. "You said we were going to wake up Arthur. You didn't say anything about waking anyone else."

"Katrinapicket, you are very ignorant," snapped Merlin. "Where would the King be without his knights? He cannot do battle single-handed."

"Battle?" queried Katrina, horrified.

"Yes," said Merlin calmly. "Here's Lancelot."

A second knight rode out of the tower. This time Katrina's heart missed two beats. His hair was as blonde as ripe cornfields, and his eyes were the colour of the Cornish sea on a sunny day: neither blue nor green but a bewitching combination of the two. Where Arthur was safe and dependable, Lancelot was magical. Sparkling. He looked such fun.

Oh... thought Katrina, looking from Lancelot to Arthur and back again. Well ... yes ... OK ... they're both amazing. No wonder Guinevere got muddled.

Lancelot greeted Merlin fondly, and then turned to Arthur. There was a slight pause as Arthur and Lancelot looked searchingly into each other's eyes. Then Katrina was surprised to see them both smile warmly and clasp each other's arm tightly. They were clearly the best of friends, whatever had happened with Guinevere.

Katrina turned just in time to see another horse emerging from the tower. A lady rode side-saddle towards them. She was radiantly beautiful with blonde hair and eyes as blue as the summer sky. Her pale green silk dress was simple and unadorned. Her crown was no more than a garland of apple blossom. Yet she was every inch a queen. Katrina could see why Merlin had found the current one disappointing. Guinevere leapt down lightly from her horse and hugged Merlin. There were tears in her eyes.

Merlin gave an embarrassed little cough and then introduced Katrina, "Squire, My Lady – Katrinapicket."

"A *female* squire? My, my, progress at last," she said, a smile flickering at the corners of her mouth. She looked at Katrina and said, "I see a courageous heart. And you will be a beauty, I think. I look forward to seeing you knighted."

Guinevere led her horse away to make room for the knights that were appearing with increasing frequency from the tower. The docks were starting to fill up with knights on horseback.

Merlin dodged the horses' teeth, but he wasn't so lucky with their other ends. He trod in a huge pile of horse dung.

"Hateful beasts," he cursed to himself. "Why can't they ride dragons instead?"

"Merlin?" hissed Katrina. "I don't understand. I thought Guinevere went off to be a nun after the big battle."

"No, no, no," said Merlin. "The books got it all wrong. She went to sleep. They *all* went to sleep. Pity really," said Merlin, looking at the knight who had now appeared in the tower doorway. "We could have done without him."

He was riding a very weedy brown horse with a scrawny neck and small mean eyes. It had little bald patches here and there, which revealed its flaky scabby skin. His armour was unpolished and his hair was unwashed. The other knights were clean-shaven, but this one had a straggly beard that had crumbs of centuries-old food stuck in it. Katrina's skin crawled as he rode towards them. He smelt of rotten fish. Of sour milk. Of bin bags that had been left out in the sun. And worse. He smelt … *evil*.

Merlin sniffed in disapproval. "Mordred," he said, nodding his head in acknowledgement. Merlin did not extend his hand.

Mordred… thought Katrina. A chill finger of fear ran down her spine. This is *Mordred*. The nasty one. The one who destroyed the Round Table. Oh help!

"Well, hello, Merlin," Mordred said in a silky, snaky voice. "And who's this?" he asked, looking Katrina up and down. "Pretty little thing… Bit young for you though, isn't she, Merlin? Or have your tastes changed over the centuries?"

Katrina felt sick.

Then suddenly Mordred's horse danced sideways and bit Merlin's arm. Merlin flinched and gritted his teeth. Mordred laughed. Katrina shuddered. Mordred spurred his horse forward to join the rear end of the group of knights.

They were like the elements, thought Katrina. There was Arthur – as trustworthy and reliable as the earth. Lancelot – as playful and lively as running water. Guinevere – as radiant and ethereal as air. And Mordred. He had an element all of his own. Mordred was slime.

Once all the knights were out of the tower – there must have been a hundred and fifty of them, Katrina reckoned – the island simply disappeared. It melted away like mist in bright sunshine. There wasn't even a ripple left in the oily green water.

King Arthur called his knights to order. "Our beloved Albion is once more in peril. We must ride again to claim the crown." Arthur's voice echoed around the docks as if it had been amplified.

There was a resounding cheer from the assembled knights. They sat on their horses expectantly, eager to follow Arthur wherever he led them.

Arthur leant forward and said in an undertone to Merlin, "Erm … Merlin… Where do we go?"

The Plan
(Sunday evening)

There was a muttered consultation on the docks. "Where does the monarch reside?" demanded Merlin.

"In London. She's at Buckingham Palace most of the time, I think," answered Katrina.

"Then to London you must go," Merlin told Arthur. "I shall join you when you wear the crown once more. Do what you must."

Arthur nodded, a serious expression setting his jaw firm. He looked around. "To London…" he said uncertainly. "To London…" His voice dropped to a deep whisper. "This place is strange to me. I know not which way London lies. Can you help me, young squire?"

Katrina gave Arthur directions, flushing pink as she gabbled, "You need to go up the M32, I think. M stands for motorway – it's like a big road. It's more or less straight across town from here. That way." She pointed roughly in the right direction. "And at the end of the road there's another motorway that goes all the way to London. Can't remember the number. Oh, and you're supposed to keep to the left-hand side. Anyway … if you follow the signs you should be alright."

"Follow the signs…" echoed Arthur in an awed voice. It was as if Katrina had said "Follow the rainbow" or "Follow the little green disappearing dwarves."

"They're not magic or anything," she explained quickly. "They just have the name of the place on them and point you in the right direction. That's all."

"How many days' ride?" asked Arthur.

"Haven't a clue," confessed Katrina. "It takes

two or three hours in the car. It's about a hundred miles, I suppose."

Arthur nodded, and smiled. Katrina's heart pounded hard within her chest. It was almost audible, and Katrina blushed again. She hoped desperately that Arthur wouldn't notice.

"Three days' ride," said Arthur to himself. "And the sun already lies low in the sky. We shall not get far before nightfall. We must away!"

He spurred his horse forward and galloped out of the docks towards the centre of Bristol. And with an almighty cheer, 150 knights thundered after him, and were gone, just as the first television crew arrived.

Katrina and Merlin slipped quietly away.

It was all over the evening news. They watched it on the television set in Merlin's room. Every channel was showing pictures of King Arthur leading his column of knights up the M32. They rode six abreast, blocking all three lanes. When they got to the end, they turned right along the M4 in the direction of London.

The traffic in the centre of Bristol and on both

motorways was brought to a complete standstill. The tailbacks ran for miles in every direction.

The newspaper and TV reporters who covered it were thrilled – they hadn't had such a good story for ages.

Arthur's miraculous appearance in the centre of Bristol didn't seem to have caused any actual alarm or panic. It was thought to be some sort of special effect – a stunning theatrical feat. It didn't seem to have occurred to anyone that it was real, live magic.

The journalists all assumed it was a protest of some sort, but he was leading his knights at such a brisk trot that nobody could run fast enough to ask him.

Each reporter had their own theory about what was going on. Most favoured the idea that Arthur was some sort of weird environmentalist, making a point about road traffic and air pollution. Some thought it was a stunt dreamt up by the Normal Theatre Company to protest about cuts in arts funding. A few linked it to the Queen's visit earlier that day, and presumed it was some sort of anti-royalist demonstration.

No one but Katrina knew the truth. The whole truth. It was a very odd feeling, and she was far from comfortable. Arthur was going to claim the crown. She didn't know quite how he would go about it, but she was sure it was going to cause an awful lot of trouble. And Merlin had said something about a battle... She didn't like the sound of that at all.

"What's going to happen?" she asked, switching off the television.

"He must challenge the false monarch and claim the crown. Do battle against her knights if necessary. Regrettable, if it comes to that, but he will do what he must. Then *he* gives me the Royal Assent, and *I* can tackle the Danger." Merlin rubbed his hands in anticipation. His black mood had completely lifted since Arthur's appearance. He was positively gleeful.

Katrina breathed out anxiously. "I'm a bit worried about this battle, really, Merlin. It's not the kind of thing they do much in England these days. The Queen's very well protected, you know. She has bodyguards, and soldiers and everything. I don't think they'll let Arthur near her."

"They are the bravest knights that ever lived," said Merlin confidently.

"You don't understand," said Katrina desperately. "They've got guns. They could kill him before he even gets a chance to talk to her. There wouldn't be a battle – not the way you mean. It wouldn't be a fair fight. They would all be shot."

Suddenly it occurred to Katrina that Merlin probably didn't know what a gun was – they wouldn't have had them last time he was awake, it would just have been swords and spears and things. And he wouldn't know about riot police and tear gas and smoke bombs – the sort of stuff that was on the news every day. "Merlin... Have you ever seen a gun?" she asked.

Merlin shook his head, but he was frowning. His eyes suddenly rolled back into his head and he fell backwards onto the bed.

Merlin was experiencing a vision.

It didn't last long, but when he came to he was visibly shocked. His face was pale and his hands were trembling.

"Blood ... blood..." he whispered. "The streets awash with blood..." Merlin met Katrina's eye. "I have seen the truth of what you say, Katrinapicket. I have seen King Arthur and all his knights lying dead. Slain. Killed from far away by men with wands of death. Guinevere too…" he shuddered.

There was a long dreadful silence.

Then Katrina asked slowly, "Merlin… Is that a vision of what *will* happen… Or is it only what *might* happen?"

"It *will* happen, Katrinapicket," said Merlin solemnly. "It will happen *if* we do nothing. We must find another way. We must concentrate, and see what we can do."

So they spent a frustrating few hours trying to think of something. Katrina kept saying things like "Suppose…?" and "What if…?" and "Do you think…?" The sentences were never finished. Uncompleted questions hung in the air unanswered. But in the end it was Katrina who came up with an idea – not a very good one, perhaps, and one that seemed most unlikely to work, but it was the only one they had. It was simple enough: to arrange a quick swap of monarchs – to replace the Queen with Arthur – just until Merlin got his

Royal Assent. It was a straightforward idea that was going to be stupendously difficult to arrange.

There was only one person who could possibly help.

The following morning, just as the sun was starting to come up, Katrina and Merlin caught a train to London. Katrina borrowed some money from Dad's wallet, and left him a note: "Taken Merlin to see Prime Minister. Don't worry. See you later. Love Kat. PS Don't tell Mum."

The Prime Minister
(Monday morning)

It had been difficult enough steering Merlin through the hazards of the Bristol streets. Getting him to London on public transport was a nightmare.

First of all there was the train. Merlin didn't understand about narrow corridors and harassed, bad-tempered commuters. He'd blocked the aisle for ages while he admired the upholstery. Katrina finally managed to get him to sit down just as the train pulled out of the station with a jolt that sent several commuters falling into the laps of several others.

Then Merlin complained loudly for what seemed like the entire journey. He stared out of the window and tutted, "Not a scrap of forest left. Not a single square inch. No dragons, no bears, no boars!"

"Bores?" the dark-suited man opposite them muttered sourly. "Train seems full of them to me…"

Once they had pulled into Paddington station, they had to negotiate their way round the Underground. Katrina would have found it difficult enough on her own, but with Merlin it was even more complicated. He found the escalators impossible to fathom. Then there were the ticket barriers and the whooshing doors.

Katrina found herself barking orders at him – "On!", "Now!", "Jump!", "Off!" – and having to shove him in the right direction. As it was, she didn't quite manage to organize them both well enough to get off at the right station. By the time she had squeezed herself and Merlin through the crush of commuters, the doors had whooshed shut. They travelled all the way round the Circle line once more. It seemed easier than getting off and working their way back.

By the time they found their way to Downing Street it was late morning. The entrance was heavily guarded. They peered through the iron railings at the end of the street. Merlin looked at the policemen. The policemen looked at Merlin. They saw an elderly man in a shabby purple dress, and they bunched together like anxious sheep.

Katrina's heart sank. She dragged Merlin back round the corner, out of sight of the policemen. "We won't even get to the front door!" she said despairingly. "All this way and we can't even get in!"

But Merlin was a sorcerer.

Pop! Pop!

There was a smell of burnt-out fireworks and Katrina felt as if she had exploded like a rocket – burst into a million fragments, which speedily reassembled themselves into a new shape. Each cell was compressed and condensed into a new body.

An uncomfortably small one.

Katrina twitched her nose. Katrina twitched her whiskers. Katrina twitched her tail.

She wasn't the hysterical type, but when she realized she was trapped inside the body of a small brown mouse, she felt decidedly queasy. She looked around for Merlin. Sitting beside her was a slightly larger mouse, with longish, greyish fur.

"Merlin?" she squeaked.

"Come on, Katrinapicket," he squeaked cheerily. "There's work to be done." And he was off, scampering between the iron railings.

Katrina had no choice. She took a deep breath (which was actually a very shallow one, given her size) and scurried along after him.

They entered Number 10 Downing Street unnoticed, when the postman delivered the mail.

Once they were inside the building, Katrina couldn't help feeling that something was very wrong. But maybe it was just that the world was a much scarier place for a small brown mouse. She was only ten centimetres long from nose to tail, so things were bound to seem a bit strange, weren't they?

They scurried along corridors, into large state-rooms and out of small offices, looking for the Prime Minister. Katrina had expected there to be a sense of purpose about the place: officials racing in all directions; computers clicking; phones ringing; fax machines whirring; people rushing around, bustling with importance; e-mails whizzing through cyberspace... But instead, it was eerily quiet. In one office a woman sat behind a desk, making a fantastically long necklace of paper clips. A man folded a document marked *Top Secret* into a paper aeroplane and flew it down the grand stair-case, missing Katrina by a whisker. Then he slid down the banister to retrieve it. Weren't these people supposed to be running the country?

Katrina and Merlin scrambled up the stairs. It was exhausting. Each step was as sheer as a cliff face. They had to dig their claws deep into the carpet to climb each one. When they reached the top of the grand staircase, it was like looking down from a mountain top. Katrina blinked nervously.

"Heights," she squeaked. "Don't like heights."

Merlin didn't hear. He was already scurrying down another corridor. He had an awful lot of energy for an old mouse, Katrina thought as she followed, her tail curled round the stitch in her side.

They found the Prime Minister. Eventually.

As they squeezed under a door at the very top of the building, Katrina and Merlin saw a pair of tartan-slippered feet at the end of a pair of pyjama-clad legs. The Prime Minister – unshaven and with very slept-in hair – was sitting on a sofa watching the lunchtime news. Katrina and Merlin scaled the back of the sofa. It was like climbing Everest.

The television was showing live pictures of traffic jams, and the column of knights advancing relentlessly along the M4. Then they flashed back to the scene that had taken place earlier that morning.

Arthur was being interviewed. Reporters were asking him questions as he prepared his horse for the day's journey.

"What is the purpose of this march?" asked one journalist.

"The kingdom is in danger," Arthur answered simply.

"You feel England is under threat?" called another.

"It is not a feeling. It is the truth. I should not have woken otherwise."

"What's the danger, Arthur? Are you protesting about the environment? Is it the air quality you're worried about?" questioned someone else.

Arthur looked at the crowd of reporters. "The air is not so sweet as it was, certainly," he answered, mounting his horse. "And the forest has been destroyed. I am sorry to see it gone. Heartily sorry." He spurred his horse forward.

"Arthur, where are you heading?" the reporters shouted in unison.

"To London."

That was it. The reporters came to the conclusion that King Arthur and his knights were a group of environmental protesters, marching on the capital to draw attention to the problems with air quality and global deforestation.

An excited-looking reporter addressed the camera. "If the convoy continues to travel at its current speed, Arthur should arrive in central London early on Wednesday morning. Government officials were unavailable for comment."

The Prime Minister shook his head and sighed deeply. "Good luck to you, Arthur. I only wish you were the real thing. We could certainly do with some magic right now…"

Pop! Pop!

Katrina exploded – burst into a million fragments – and, to her great relief, found herself back in her spacious and roomy body. She felt a little dizzy.

She was sitting on the sofa beside the Prime Minister. He didn't shout, or call for help. But that may have been because Merlin had transformed right on top of him and had enveloped him in the folds of his velvet dress.

They pulled apart, eventually, and Merlin apologized for his "minor miscalculation".

The Prime Minister remained very calm. Suspiciously calm. Desperately calm. Katrina remembered feeling like that when she had been stuck to the cave roof. It was the eerie calmness of someone for whom things couldn't possibly get worse. What on earth was going on?

"Let me guess," said the Prime Minister, his eyes glazed and unfocussed. He was looking through Merlin as if he was a ghost. "You're Merlin. Of course. Well, it's probably about time you appeared. Jolly good."

Only then did the Prime Minister become aware of Katrina. He seemed puzzled by her presence and waved his arm vaguely in her direction, as if he was trying to rub her out. When she didn't disappear, he asked Merlin, "Who's that?"

"My squire," answered Merlin. "Katrinapicket."

The Prime Minister looked baffled. "Hmmm," he said to himself. "Strange what the subconscious mind drags in." He looked at Merlin and Katrina. "Good morning to you both. I suppose you've come to save Albion?" He didn't wait for an answer. "Good, good. Well, off you go then. Don't let me stand in your way. Albion needs all the help she can get."

There was a knock on the door.

Pop! Pop! Merlin transformed himself and Katrina back into mice.

"Not again!" Katrina shouted, but no one heard her. By the time she protested, she was already a mouse.

"Sir? Have you had a chance to give some thought to the teachers' pay claim?" An official looking man stood in the doorway.

"Give them the money," said the Prime Minister, with an airy wave of his hand. "Everything they ask for. More. Double it. Triple it. Starting Thursday." He gave a high, hysterical titter.

"Very well, sir," said the official, with a frown of concern.

A worried looking woman appeared beside him. "Sir, I have the President of the United States on the phone."

"Oh really?" said the Prime Minister. "Well you can tell him to go boil his head." He started to giggle to himself.

"I'll tell him you're not available," she sniffed.

The officials exchanged anxious glances and closed the door.

Pop! Pop!

"If you do that to me again," snapped Katrina, "I'll be sick."

Merlin wasn't listening. He was staring at the Prime Minister. "The man's cracking up," he said in disgust. "I've seen it all before."

"You still here?" said the Prime Minister. "Don't let me keep you. Off you go. Do your stuff. Save the kingdom. Heaven knows it needs it."

Katrina thought it was time to intervene. "We need your help," she began.

"They all say that," he replied. "But there's nothing I can do now. Nothing, nothing, nothing, nothing, nothing."

Merlin got cross. "Pull yourself together, man. Albion is in Peril."

"Oh, yes, I know…" said the Prime Minister, in a sing-song voice. "But I can't help it. Nothing I can do. Nothing at all, at all, at all. Nothing, nothing, nothing, noth—"

Thwack!

Katrina gasped. Merlin had slapped the Prime Minister. *Slapped* him. The *Prime Minister*.

"The danger is fast approaching from the heavens," said Merlin angrily. "The kingdom will be engulfed in flames. I shall save Albion. We just need a little assistance."

The Prime Minister shook his head as if he had been swimming underwater and was trying to get the water out of his ears. His eyes focussed on Merlin for the first time. "Are you *really* here?" he asked.

"Of course I'm *here!*" Merlin exploded.

"I thought I was imagining you... Felt I was going stark raving mad..." The Prime Minister's eyes narrowed. "You *know* what's on its way?"

Merlin nodded.

"You *really* think something can be done about it?" the Prime Minister asked.

"Indeed," Merlin assured him.

The Prime Minister stiffened. There was a glimmer of hope in his eyes. "Do you have a plan?" he asked.

Katrina couldn't stay silent for a moment longer. "How come *you* know about it?" she demanded.

The Prime Minister looked at her. "There are hundreds of scientists working for the Government, you know," he answered flatly. "One of them spotted the meteorite last week. A huge great flaming lump of rock the size of a house that's going to land on England. It will probably wipe out the entire country. Maybe take a bit of France too. Who knows what it will do to the rest of the planet? That's what killed off the dinosaurs, after all."

Katrina's mouth hung open. "But you haven't

done anything," she protested.

"No ... well." The Prime Minister scratched his head and said helplessly, "There's nothing *to* be done. And there didn't seem any *point* causing total panic. I ordered the scientific lot to keep quiet. And I've given strict instructions that everything should carry on as normal until the end of the world. Which will be lunchtime on Wednesday, according to the experts."

"Wednesday," muttered Merlin under his breath. "I *felt* it must be so."

"*Wednesday*?" exploded Katrina. "*Wednesday*! That's in *two days*!"

The Prime Minister nodded gravely. He looked hard at Merlin, took in the windswept hair, the faded velvet dress. He swallowed nervously. Then he said, "I'm terribly sorry... I've been in a bit of a state lately... Were you really a mouse when you came in, or did I imagine it?"

"No, you're quite right," Merlin answered. "Best way in, you see."

"Well... Merlin..." The Prime Minister scratched his head again, trying to take it all in. "Merlin... *Merlin!* Gosh!" Suddenly he grasped Merlin's hand

and pumped it up and down enthusiastically.

Merlin looked confused. They obviously hadn't gone in for hand shaking in his day, thought Katrina.

"I am *very* glad to meet you," continued the Prime Minister. "Amazing! I was never sure if you had really existed, you know. And I always thought it was a myth – you waking up again. I am very glad indeed to find that I was wrong." Hope gleamed in his eyes. "Tell me what I can do to help you."

Feeding Arthur
(Monday afternoon)

The Prime Minister sat and listened and made notes while Merlin outlined Katrina's idea. It didn't take long.

There was a weighty pause while the Prime Minister sat with furrowed eyebrows.

Eventually he said, "A temporary substitution of monarchs... Hmmm..." He stood up and began to pace up and down the room. "I shall have to obtain the crown by some sort of subterfuge. Perhaps I could have it removed for cleaning... Then a discreet little rendezvous with the Archbishop first thing Wednesday morning. A secret ceremony at the Abbey. No one need know anything about it. It can be done just as soon as Arthur gets into London. Then pop the crown back and no one's any the wiser." He rubbed his temples. "It's going to be difficult – the timing will be a *nightmare*. But then," he said airily, as if he did it every day, "saving the world is always a tricky business, isn't it? I shall telephone the Archbishop this afternoon. But first let's get some food sorted out for all those knights. They must be terribly peckish by now…"

His sense of being-in-control restored, the Prime Minister (who was still in his pyjamas) swung into action. Officials raced in all directions; computers clicked, phones rang and fax machines whirred; e-mails whizzed through cyberspace.

Within the hour, a lorry loaded with provisions pulled up at the end of Downing Street. Food, beer and wine, oats and hay for the horses, blankets – everything they had been able to think of that would make the knights' journey more comfortable was stuffed into the lorry. Katrina and Merlin would ride in the cab with the driver so they could meet Arthur and tell him the plan. The lorry was then going to take them home to Bristol before Katrina's mum started panicking about where Katrina had got to.

The Prime Minister bade them a fond farewell, pumping Merlin's hand again and then patting Katrina on the head affectionately.

"I shall see you in two days' time," he said. "On the steps of Westminster Abbey, if all goes according to plan."

"Make sure it does," Merlin answered darkly. "The fate of Albion depends on it..."

By the time Katrina and Merlin reached them, Arthur and his knights were extremely hungry. They had camped overnight in a field a few miles west of Swindon. But there was no forest, therefore no wild boar to hunt, therefore nothing to cook and nothing to eat. Mordred was the only one who had complained. The rest of the knights were bold, brave and true, and had quietly lain down to sleep, with only their stomachs grumbling. It was fortunate that they hadn't spotted the field of cows just over the hill. Killing a cow by the side of the road could have turned people against them.

As it was, they were attracting a lot of support, despite the traffic chaos. People were joining the march on London. All sorts of protest groups had started to follow the knights. There were environmentalists and anti-road protesters, evangelists and anarchists. Every weird and wonderful fringe campaign group seemed to be there, waving flags, wearing badges, singing slogans. And there were

hundreds of sightseers too who'd come to see the splendid procession.

Guinevere rode between Lancelot and Arthur at the head of a column of knights. They looked magnificent. Mordred trailed along at the back, sniping and moaning and sowing seeds of discord. People tried hard to ignore him, but he was like a disease; infecting the air around him with bitterness and bad temper.

*   *   *

The lorry carrying Katrina and Merlin followed a police escort up the hard shoulder on the wrong side of the motorway to avoid the traffic jam. It reached Arthur and his knights at teatime, and that evening – on the grass verge of the M4, just outside Reading – they feasted for the first time in centuries.

It was an amazingly festive occasion. With the prospect of battle averted, there was a party-like atmosphere. Lancelot moved amongst the crowd, spreading warmth and good humour as thickly as Merlin spread his marmalade. And the love that flowed between Arthur, Guinevere and Lancelot crackled like a force field, holding everyone in its charmed embrace. They were the three equal sides of a triangle, Katrina thought – each one balancing the other two – none of them complete without the others.

The knights were happy – laughing and telling jokes and stories. It was contagious. Katrina caught the happy mood, handing out provisions from the back of the lorry with a broad smile creasing her face. Somehow she pushed the image of a lump of flaming rock to the back of her mind.

Merlin drew Arthur quietly aside to fill him in on the arrangements made by the Prime Minister, while the rest of the knights fell on the food with gusto followed by embarrassed confusion. One after the other the knights were defeated by the mysteries of modern packaging. They wandered up and down the hard shoulder, shaking unopened drinks cartons and biting shrink-wrapped roast chicken legs in utter bafflement. There was nearly a nasty incident when one frustrated knight took his sword to a can of Coke. Katrina stopped him just as he was about to slice it in two. She demonstrated the ring pull and the knight stared at her as if she had accomplished a feat of real magic. After that, they all came to her, one at a time. Katrina spent the next two hours opening crisp packets, unscrewing bottle tops and peeling the foil off bars of chocolate.

She helped everyone but Mordred.

He sidled up to her and said, in a sneering slimy voice, "Open this for me. Mind you, it hardly seems worth it. It's not what I'd call food. Is this the best Merlin could come up with? Pathetic."

"Do it yourself," snapped Katrina. She turned her back on him.

But she couldn't help hearing the jibe he threw at her.

"Merlin won't make any difference, you know," he sneered. "He couldn't save the kingdom last time so why should he succeed now? He's useless. Totally useless."

Mordred's parting shot hit its mark. Katrina sat in the back of the lorry and watched Merlin. He looked worried. He was still talking to Arthur, but every now and then he squinted up at the darkening sky and his brow furrowed with anxiety. Katrina realized with a sudden jolt of fear that they'd only made *half* a plan. They'd found a way of getting the Royal Assent, but what happened *after* that? How on earth was Merlin going to deal with the meteorite?

At last Merlin walked back to the lorry with Arthur. Arthur smiled at her, and Katrina was very glad she was sitting down: her knees seemed to have gone all wobbly.

"A fair day's work, young squire," said Arthur in

his deep warm voice. "Albion shall have much to thank you for."

Katrina mumbled a squeaky, "Thank you," and flushed scarlet.

When the knights had eaten their fill, the lorry driver took Katrina and Merlin back home to Bristol.

"I need to get within range," muttered Merlin to himself. "I must intercept the Peril before it strikes Albion." Merlin eyed the sky once more. Then he sank into a preoccupied silence for the rest of the journey.

It was only when they arrived back at Katrina's house that Merlin finally spoke to Katrina.

"I have it!" he cried suddenly.

Merlin turned to Katrina with excitement burning in his eyes.

"Katrinapicket, we must find a dragon!"

Finding Desmond
(Tuesday morning)

The following morning, just as the sun was starting to streak the sky with shreds of pink and gold, Merlin shook Katrina awake.

"Whasamaddernow?" she mumbled sleepily.

"I've had an idea," said Merlin. "I know where to find him."

"Who?"

"Desmond."

"*Who?*"

"*Desmond,*" said Merlin reproachfully. "Katrinapicket, you have not been paying attention. Desmond – my dragon friend. The one who's fond of chess. Don't you remember?"

Katrina sat up in bed. "Do I have to do another invocation?" she asked, rubbing her eyes.

"No, no. I can bring him here without that. Come on, Katrinapicket, up you get."

"You're not going to do a transformation, are you?" Katrina was suddenly nervous. She was unwilling to leave the safety of her bedroom if Merlin was going to change himself into a man-eating dragon – or worse – transform *her* into one.

"No, no, no," said Merlin irritably. "You are not *listening*, Katrinapicket. I can find him. He's *here*, I think. Let us go and see if my theory is correct."

Reluctantly, anxiously, Katrina stumbled along in Merlin's wake as he marched through the deserted Bristol streets.

"I've been thinking, you see?" said Merlin. "About dragons. He was very resourceful, was Desmond. A cut above your average fire breather. I was thinking, if any of them has survived the deforestation of Albion it will be him. And I

113

started wondering how he might have done it – survived without being noticed. I mean, a big creature like him roaring around the place – bound to get spotted, you see? How could he have stayed alive? And then the answer came to me..." He looked at Katrina triumphantly. "By pretending not to be, of course!"

It was too early, and Katrina had had too little sleep for her to understand what on earth Merlin was talking about. "Pretending not to be what?" she asked.

"Not to be alive!" Merlin was very excited; his eyes were shining.

Katrina still didn't understand. "Not alive?" she echoed. "What? Dead?"

"No!" said Merlin, exasperated. "Not dead. Just not alive!"

Katrina looked blank.

"A dragon could survive by pretending not to be alive. He could live in full view. Everyone would ignore him, you see? Or give him only a passing glance. If he pretended he was a replica ... a representation ... a statue. A statue, Katrinapicket, don't you see? A statue."

They rounded the corner, and there it was: the new art gallery that the Queen had opened a couple of days before. The pink sky was reflected in its mirrored surfaces, and clouds – outlined in gold by the rising sun – drifted prettily across it. And next to the art gallery – large, motionless, badly painted, and very obviously made of fibreglass – stood the dragon.

He's flipped, Katrina thought, with a sinking feeling in the pit of her stomach. A huge great meteorite is going to hit us tomorrow lunchtime and Merlin's flipped. Oh, help!

Merlin marched up to the statue purposefully and said loudly, "Desmond! It is I, Merlin!"

Nothing.

"Make yourself known."

Nothing.

"Reveal yourself!"

Still nothing.

"Oh, come on, Desmond," said Merlin, in a wheedling tone now. "It's me, *Merlin*. You remember *me*, don't you, old friend?"

Still nothing.

"He's sulking," said Merlin. "Because I beat him

115

last time we played chess."

Katrina thought it was time to intervene. "It's a *statue*, Merlin. It isn't *real*. Look!" She banged hard on the dragon's stomach. It was cold and hard and there was an echoing sound deep within the creature. "See?" Katrina said firmly. "It's plastic. Totally hollow."

Merlin touched the dragon's scales. His face fell. He was crushed with disappointment. Tears brightened his eyes and his voice went all wobbly. "I was so sure…" he said. "Oh, Katrinapicket, what are we to do?" For the first time, Merlin looked old and tired and helpless.

Katrina started to lead him away gently by the arm. She felt numb. If *Merlin* didn't know what to do, what hope was left?

They hadn't got very far across the street when they heard something. A soft slither of scales. A whisper of wings. The *thump!* of a very large creature sitting down hard.

"*Hollow*," said a sulky voice behind them. "Of course I'm *hollow*. I haven't had anyone to eat for *centuries*."

Merlin and Katrina spun round.

116

The dragon – Desmond – was sitting watching them, with his wings folded neatly across his back. "And *I* won the last game of chess, not you," he said. "You were so besotted with that Nimue creature you couldn't even think straight." Desmond tutted and shook his head. A little puff of smoke snorted through his nostrils.

Katrina's mouth fell open.

"Catch flies in that if you're not careful," said Desmond.

Katrina shut her mouth, and watched, eyes wide, as Merlin bowed deeply in front of Desmond.

"Bow, Katrinapicket," Merlin hissed out of the corner of his mouth. "You need to show respect for dragons. Bow, or you'll be his next meal."

Hastily, and not very gracefully, Katrina bowed low.

"That's better," Desmond sniffed. He did seem to be in a very bad mood. But that was hardly surprising if he had to spend so much time standing motionless pretending to be a statue.

"Sorry," said Katrina. "It was the paint, you see. I didn't think you were real."

"Oh, that," said Desmond carelessly. "Applied it myself. Didn't want to look too realistic. Attracts attention. Best to look a bit vulgar. People don't look too closely then."

Merlin cleared his throat. "So... Desmond... How are you?" Merlin wasn't very good at polite conversation. He smiled awkwardly.

"I've been better," said Desmond, darkly.

"But you've been ... managing ... have you?"

"If you can call it managing," grumbled Desmond. "Living on scraps – leftovers. Standing around all day. Not what you'd call a life, is it?"

"No ... no ... I suppose not..." Merlin had had enough social chitchat. He cut straight to the point. "I need your help," he said bluntly.

"Huh!" sniffed Desmond. "Thought there would be *something*. Knew you wouldn't bother otherwise."

"Albion is in peril," persisted Merlin. "We need your help to save the kingdom."

"Don't know if it's worth saving," said Desmond, grumpily. "All the forest gone. So many people you can hardly move. And there's barely a dragon left, you know." He paused and then said sadly, "Do you remember the Prendergasts?"

Merlin nodded.

"Charming family," continued Desmond. "Muriel and Brian and little Egbert. Living quietly in Surrey, minding their own business…"

"I seem to recall that Brian was rather hot-tempered," Merlin interrupted tactlessly.

"Hot-tempered? Of course he was hot-tempered! He was a dragon! What do you expect? Bound to be a tad incendiary now and again." Desmond snorted in disgust. Jets of flame burst from both nostrils, hitting the road a few metres away and burning a neat hole in the tarmac. "It was terrible what happened to them. Trifling little fire on the cathedral roof and the Archbishop called in the dragon exterminators. Poor little Egbert was left an orphan. Tragic it was. Tragic."

"Indeed," Merlin said, nodding in agreement. "And what became of Egbert?"

"Moved to London. Lived on Hampstead Heath for a while. Then he had that unfortunate sneezing fit in Pudding Lane, set fire to the bakery. He had to go north after that. We've lost touch. It's not easy to communicate these days, you know. Don't know where he is now."

Desmond heaved a deep sigh. Warm smoke wreathed around Katrina's ankles.

"It's not been much fun lately," moaned Desmond.

"Well, I'm sure we can do something about that," said Merlin optimistically. "But first of all, I require your services."

Desmond grunted dismissively.

"Arthur's helping," Katrina spoke without thinking. "I summoned him and his knights."

There was a very long silence. Desmond fixed Katrina with a searching gaze and looked her up and down very slowly. Very thoroughly. Inch by hot embarrassed inch. A sliver of fear prickled down Katrina's spine: Desmond appeared to be licking his lips. He began to pick his teeth with one extremely long claw.

"You did, did you?" he said at last. His tone was thoughtful. "Summoned Arthur … hmmmmm." He dislodged something from a rear molar. It plopped wetly onto the paving. It could have been the remains of a shoe.

"Lancelot?" Desmond asked casually.

"Lancelot," confirmed Merlin. He raised his eyebrows and added pointedly, "And Guinevere."

At the mention of Guinevere's name, Desmond's wings gave a little involuntary flutter. He might have been blushing. Katrina stared. There was a definite flush of pink shimmering across his scales.

"The whole fellowship has returned," continued Merlin. "They advance on London even as we speak."

"*All* of them?" Desmond's eyes narrowed to thin slits.

"*All* of them," Merlin's tone was flat, neutral.

Katrina didn't understand what the exchange meant, but she was sure it meant something. It was as if some sort of bargain had been struck.

Desmond glanced around the harbour, considering, sucking his teeth noisily. Then he gave Katrina a long hard stare, which she met squarely, even though she was quivering inside.

"I'll do it," he announced at last. "On one condition."

"What might that be?" said Merlin.

"It's private," said Desmond. "I don't want *her* to hear."

Merlin approached Desmond, and Desmond whispered something in his ear. Merlin flushed.

Looked at Katrina. Nodded his head.

"I'm sure that can be arranged," he said. Katrina didn't like the sound of that at all.

Merlin made arrangements with Desmond to meet at the crack of dawn the following day. But for now the safest thing seemed to be for the dragon to resume his position – up on his hind legs, wings outstretched, mouth slightly open revealing very large, very sharp teeth.

"See you in the morning," Desmond whispered. "Wednesday..."

Katrina and Merlin made their way back home for breakfast. Katrina let them in with her front door key and they headed sleepily for the kitchen.

"Toast and marmalade?" she asked.

"That would be most welcome," said Merlin.

Katrina opened the door and stopped in her tracks. A tanned young man was sitting at the table with a cup of tea in front of him.

It was Adrian, her brother, back from Australia.

Standing next to him – arms folded, tight-lipped, with a face like thunder – was her mother.

Dad was nowhere to be seen. He had obviously

left for work early, perhaps sensing the approaching storm.

"So," said Mum, her foot tapping the floor like a rhinoceros about to charge. "There's me thinking you're one of the Normal Theatre lot, and now I discover they've never even heard of you. Who are you really, Merlin?"

"Merlin," said Merlin innocently. He may have been the most powerful sorcerer that ever lived, but he knew precious little about how dangerous mothers can be when they find out they have been tricked.

"Merlin..." said Mum, through gritted teeth. "Ha ... ha ... ha."

She looked at Katrina. "And what on earth do you think you've been doing, young lady? Out all day yesterday! Not home until gone midnight! Running around with a madman from who knows where! I only let him stay because I thought he was one of Adrian's lot."

"I never *told* you that," said Katrina.

Mum's voice was icy calm. "But you let me believe it, didn't you?"

Katrina said nothing. It didn't seem the right

time to start explaining about the meteorite.

Adrian studied his teacup very carefully, as if he had never seen one before.

Merlin, completely oblivious to the mounting domestic tension, sat down happily in a chair and said, "Well, Lady Mymum, I think I shall have some toast and marmalade now."

He got it. Mum delivered it to him full in the face, slapping it into his nose like a custard pie.

Then she exploded. The torrent of words seemed to go on forever. It ended with a threat to call the police to inform them there was a dangerous lunatic wandering the streets of Bristol pretending to be a wizard.

"Sorcerer," corrected Merlin huffily, through his sticky, marmalade-smeared beard.

Mum strode out of the kitchen, wrenched the front door open, marched back into the kitchen and ordered Merlin to leave.

"If you ever come near Katrina again, I'll—" Mum suddenly fell silent.

Katrina looked up. Her mum was standing stock still, mouth open mid-sentence. She was motionless. Frozen.

Katrina looked at Adrian. He was frozen too, teacup halfway to his lips. She turned to Merlin. "What have you done?" she asked in horror.

"Regrettable," he said sadly. "Very regrettable. Sorry, Katrinapicket, but I really had no choice. I think we had better go and join Arthur before we suffer any other unforeseen interruptions."

"But what's happened?" Katrina asked. "Will they be alright?"

"Oh, yes," said Merlin. "Minor magic, that's all. No harm has been done. They're frozen in time until we restart them. Which, all being well, will be after the Danger has passed."

Katrina left a note pinned to her mother.

"Dear Dad," it said. "Sorry about Mum and Adrian. Merlin says he'll be back to unfreeze them on Thursday morning. Gone to sort out the Danger. Don't worry. Love Kat. PS Don't try to move them or anything – Merlin says it's best to leave them where they are."

A Night in the Open
(Tuesday evening)

The sight of a dragon trotting down the hard shoulder of the M4 hadn't caused nearly as much of a stir as Katrina had expected. She and Merlin rode on Desmond's back – he had a dent at the base of his neck that was large enough to accommodate them both comfortably. It was a bit like being carried along on a moulded plastic sofa.

Stranded motorists regarded the spectacle as a pleasant diversion from the tedium of a hundred-mile-long traffic jam. Nobody seemed to realize he was a real live dragon. They all treated Desmond as if he was a particularly elaborate carnival float. People smiled and pointed and nudged each other in the ribs. Desmond called cheerful "hellos" in reply, and Merlin waved regally. The sun shone, and it would have been a wonderful journey for Katrina if it hadn't been for the menacing rumble of a very large, very empty stomach.

"How do dragons choose who they eat?" Katrina whispered.

"For heaven's sake, Katrinapicket!" said Merlin. "The Danger is almost upon us! Have you nothing better to think of than Desmond's dietary requirements?"

Merlin didn't quite meet her eyes. Katrina continued to feel anxious.

Desmond could travel twice as fast as a horse, in half the time, but even so they didn't reach Arthur until well after dark. He had set up camp in a park at the end of the motorway. By the time Desmond trotted through the gates, most of the knights had already settled down to sleep.

Desmond had cheered up no end. He was like a

different dragon. He had whistled jauntily between his sharp teeth for most of the journey. When Katrina slithered down off his back, Desmond beamed at her fondly. His new-found affection for Katrina was making her very nervous.

Arthur greeted Desmond with a low, stately bow.

"My thanks to you, Lord Dragon. I am honoured indeed that such a splendid creature should come to the aid of Albion!"

Desmond gave a rich throaty chuckle and puffed a little cloud of smoke around Arthur by way of reply. He was clearly delighted by Arthur's flattery.

Katrina and Merlin ate a small supper of bread and bits of cheese left over from the knights' meal. Desmond ate everything else he could find, including the packaging. Then he curled round a convenient tree, closed his eyes and almost immediately started to snore. Merlin lay down next to him, resting his head on one of Desmond's claws, and soon he was snoring too.

Katrina wrapped a blanket around herself and settled down on the grass. She tried to sleep, but the ground was horribly hard. The knights didn't

seem to mind: they were used to sleeping in the open air. All around her Katrina could hear deep gentle breathing. But Katrina – who was accustomed to the comfort of a springy mattress, not to mention four walls and a roof over her head – lay awake and worried.

There was plenty to worry about.

It had been a very peculiar week, thought Katrina. She seemed to have set off a chain of events over which she had no control. But why *her*? Why had *she* been the one to do it? It was a scary feeling. She was the only person in England who knew it was all for real – that Arthur and his knights were genuine, not actors pretending. Well … her and the Prime Minister. And Dad – Dad must know, deep down, even if he would never admit it. She thought of Dad with a pang of guilt: imagined him eating his tea in the kitchen with the motionless bodies of Mum and Adrian. Poor Dad. He'd probably spend the entire night in the shed… Maybe he'd be so upset that he'd never ever come out again. It would be all her fault.

And there was this dragon to worry about. A dragon whose stomach had rumbled loudly the entire length of the M4. A dragon who kept looking at her in the longing way Mum looked at chocolates when she was on a diet.

She didn't want to think about it.

Katrina wriggled around, in an attempt to get comfortable. She should never have gone down that pothole, she thought to herself. Then none of it would have happened... But then, suppose she hadn't? What would the future have been then? She lay on her back, gazing up at the stars. One of those pinpricks of light was heading their way. One of those glowing dots was bringing death and destruction and disaster. Which one of them was targeted on England?

And suppose Merlin's plan didn't work?

The thought sat like a ball of ice in the pit of her stomach. Suppose Mordred was right? Merlin hadn't managed to change anything last time he was awake, had he? The Round Table had collapsed despite his warnings. He hadn't been able to do a thing to change the course of history. Mum's words echoed in her memory, "It all ended in disaster. It was an absolute bloodbath."

What would happen if Merlin failed?

She *definitely* didn't want to think about *that*.

Katrina curled up into a tight ball and tried to push away the thoughts that were circling round and round in her mind. It wasn't until just before dawn that Katrina fell into a light, uneasy sleep.

Crowning Arthur
(Wednesday morning)

At 7 o'clock on Wednesday morning, Katrina Picket rode into London on a dragon. Arthur had insisted she lead the way, on the grounds that she and Desmond knew more about modern-day London than anyone else. Merlin was sitting behind her. Arthur, Guinevere, Lancelot and a column of knights cantered behind, hooves clattering loudly on the London streets, armour glinting in the morning sun.

Mordred brought up the rear, grumbling and

complaining to anyone within earshot, "Merlin's gone mad. I don't know why he bothered to wake us up. This is never going to work."

Merlin had arranged to meet the Prime Minister outside Westminster Abbey, but neither Katrina nor Desmond knew how to get there. So Desmond stopped outside the first petrol station they came to, and Katrina climbed down. She nipped into the shop, bought a London A-Z, and then climbed back up onto Desmond's back.

With the map in her hand, Katrina issued directions: "Left at the roundabout... Get in the right-hand lane... Straight across here." They clattered over the Hammersmith flyover and up the Cromwell Road.

After that, it became more complicated. It wasn't easy, map-reading from the back of a speeding dragon. The wind kept blowing the pages around, and the bit she wanted to look at always seemed to be in the fold of the map. And there were so many roads to choose from. At least on the Underground everything had been neatly colour-coded, with nice straight lines to follow. The map was a mess of wiggly bits and tiny writing. Katrina didn't have a clue which was the best route to take. In the end, she directed Desmond up and down streets whose names were vaguely familiar, hoping that the strange and mysterious force that had led her to Merlin in the first place might be plotting out the route for her. She realized later that it had had nothing to do with destiny – she had simply recognized names off the Monopoly board. They thundered up Park Lane and twice round Marble Arch before Katrina realized they were heading in the wrong direction. Back down through Mayfair, along Piccadilly and Regent Street and into Pall Mall. The roads were clear – inner London had been closed off to traffic by prime ministerial command – but well-wishers and sightseers lined the streets, waving and cheering and calling out words of encouragement. Katrina realized with a sinking feeling that this wasn't going to be the discreet little rendezvous that the Prime Minister had planned. She hoped he was going to manage.

At the end of Pall Mall, Desmond galloped into Trafalgar Square. There was a tremendous clatter of hooves behind them. Katrina looked over her shoulder – some of the knights' horses had been spooked when they had spotted the lion statues at the foot of Nelson's Column. Desmond came to a standstill while the knights regained control of their horses and re-organized themselves.

Katrina looked around Trafalgar Square. There was no getting away from it – London was amazing. Everything was so ... so *big*. It was on a different scale to Bristol: as if Bristol had been constructed from the tiniest Lego bricks and London had been manufactured from chunky Duplo. Both cities were grand, but the buildings in London all seemed ten times the size of the ones in Bristol and ten times more splendid.

"What an extraordinary edifice," said Merlin, staring up at Nelson's Column. "What did that knight do to deserve such a monument?"

"Er ... not sure," said Katrina. "Won a battle, I think."

"Humph," Merlin tutted. "Wars! You'd think there would be better things to remember..."

Katrina didn't catch the rest of his comment. The knights had got themselves sorted out and Desmond was off again, speeding down Whitehall towards the Houses of Parliament.

*   *   *

At 9 a.m. Katrina Picket, Merlin, an enormous dragon, King Arthur, Lancelot, Guinevere and 150 mounted knights in gleaming armour arrived outside Westminster Abbey.

The Prime Minister was already there, and he was not alone. An army of journalists was assembled around the Abbey, cameras and flashguns pointed threateningly in their direction.

When the Prime Minister came down the steps to greet them, he smiled widely for the photographers. If he was surprised by Desmond, he didn't show it. He shook Merlin warmly by the hand and bowed to Arthur. Desmond assumed the bow was meant for him (which was probably just as well) and puffed a wreath of smoke, which settled briefly round the Prime Minister's shoulders. The Prime Minister kissed Guinevere on both cheeks, blushed fiercely, and did it again. Then he patted Katrina on the head.

The plan seemed to have taken a different shape, and neither Merlin nor Katrina knew quite what to do next. Arthur and his knights hovered uncertainly on the steps, wondering what was expected of them.

The Prime Minister took control. He made a speech.

"Ladies and gentlemen, I know that there has been a great deal of speculation in the press about King Arthur's ride on London. But today I can reveal that this has not been a protest march. I can now tell you all that this has been a surprise arranged to commemorate the Queen's jubilee. It has been a march of celebration.

"One legendary monarch – our very own King Arthur – has ridden across England to pay tribute to our own dear Queen. In this, the year of her jubilee, he has made a triumphant journey that ends here at Westminster Abbey.

"Our celebrations on this special surprise public holiday begin with a coronation ceremony."

The Prime Minister looked at King Arthur, and said, for his benefit as much as for the reporters, "King Arthur will be crowned here in the Abbey. It is a symbolic moment. He will then *hand the crown back* to the Queen, thus showing the continuity of the monarchy, from early times to the present day."

Then he looked at Merlin and Katrina. "At around lunchtime, there will be a spectacular display of fireworks and ... er ... other ... *things* ... in the skies over London."

Merlin looked up. The meteorite was now just visible to the naked eye – it was a pinprick of light glowing in the sky like an unusually bright star. A star visible in daylight – glinting with strange menace. "A bit earlier, I think," he hissed to the Prime Minister. "Hurry it all up a bit."

The Prime Minister paled visibly, but remembered to throw a terrific beaming smile at the photographers and hurried into the Abbey. Arthur, Guinevere, Lancelot and all the knights followed, armour clanking. They left their horses munching the grass in Parliament Square.

Katrina was amazed. It was supposed to have been a quick swap of monarchs. A temporary substitution. The Archbishop was supposed to have run in, dropped the crown on Arthur's head and said the necessary words. Then Merlin could have got his Royal Assent and they would have been off without anyone knowing. But now it had turned into a huge public event, like the Trooping of the Colour, or a royal wedding.

I suppose it all got a bit out of hand, Katrina

thought. Arthur's ride had created such traffic chaos and got so much public support that the Prime Minister had been forced to give some sort of explanation. And he had certainly made the most of it. It was almost like he was taking advantage of the publicity... And declaring a day's special public holiday was bound to make him popular. He had an eye to the future – if it came.

Cars started to pull up outside the Abbey, and out climbed politicians, pop stars, film stars, television stars, footballers with their supermodel wives. It seemed that every famous person in England had turned out for this grand occasion.

They were followed by marching bands, horse-drawn coaches, and at last the Queen herself. Her coach seemed to be made of solid gold. It had ruby red velvet upholstery and was drawn by eight immaculately groomed white horses. It was dazzling, like something out of a fairy tale. The Queen was looking splendid in full royal regalia, jewels flashing in the sunshine.

"Ah, yes," said Merlin approvingly. "*That's* more like it."

The crown was carried before the Queen by a

small pageboy. As she mounted the steps to the Abbey, the Queen froze for a second and stared hard at Katrina. Then she continued on her way into the Abbey. Katrina overheard her say to her husband, "Hiy ixtraordinirry! Thit's the vintriliquist I tild yew abite."

Katrina and Merlin watched the ceremony from outside the Abbey on a live video link up. They could see every detail on the big screen.

The light in the sky was getting brighter by the minute, and Merlin was tense and fidgety. "Hurry up ... hurry up..." he muttered to himself.

Inside the Abbey, Arthur was in his place. He knelt at the altar, with Guinevere on his left, and Lancelot on his right.

The Queen followed the pageboy up the aisle, at a calm, dignified, regal pace, and then stood at the left of the altar.

Then everyone sang "Land of Hope and Glory". Very slowly.

Outside, Merlin was hopping from foot to foot. "Come on ... come on!" he muttered.

Katrina sat on the steps of the Abbey, arms folded

tight across her chest, fear gnawing her insides.

Inside the Abbey, they got to the last verse.

"What is this interminable dirge?" Merlin exploded angrily. "The Peril is almost upon us!"

Now the Archbishop was making a speech about the monarchy, and the guardianship of the kingdom. It was pretty much the same as Merlin had said to Katrina. Only longer. Much, much longer. He went on ... and on ... and on.

Katrina clasped her arms around her knees and buried her face, bunching herself into a tight, terrified ball. She felt as if her stomach was trying to climb out of her throat. Merlin was biting his fingernails, practically gnawing his fingers to the bone. His face was white and he kept looking anxiously at the sky.

The pinprick of light had been getting steadily bigger. It was now the size of a marble.

The Archbishop finished his speech. Arthur sat on the throne. The Archbishop took the crown. He raised it over Arthur's head. He said more words. Katrina couldn't hear what they were because Merlin was screeching in her ear.

"Look, Katrinapicket! Look!" he yelled.

She looked.

The marble-sized ball of light was now as big as a golf ball. Suddenly it changed colour. It glowed orange – the colour of fire. It had entered the earth's atmosphere. It grew to the size of a tennis ball as she watched.

The Archbishop placed the crown on Arthur's head.

Arthur leapt from the throne, knocking the Archbishop off balance and sending him spinning down the aisle of the Abbey.

"I grant Royal Assent!" Arthur bellowed so loudly that they could hear him outside even without the video link. "Merlin – do what you must!"

Fireballs and Flying Dragons

(Wednesday midday)

With a speed that astonished even Katrina, Merlin leapt onto Desmond's back. "Come on, Katrinapicket!" he shouted.

"Me?" she squeaked. "I can't go up there – I'm scared of heights!" It hadn't occurred to her that Merlin would want her to go with him.

"Katrinapicket..." Merlin's voice was suddenly calm and earnest. "You are the sorceress who woke me. You are the sorceress who summoned Arthur. You are the sorceress who stopped Desmond sulking.

We cannot complete this task without you."

Her whole being screamed against it. Katrina was terrified. Utterly terrified.

But then Mordred was beside her on the steps of the Abbey, a withering sneer contorting his face. "*Her?*" he spat in contempt. "You need *her?* Look at her! She's scared stiff!"

Katrina didn't say a word. She couldn't speak. She was overcome with blind fury. And an absolute determination to do whatever she had to – however petrifying.

Katrina didn't know quite how she managed it, but suddenly there she was. On Desmond's back. And he was unfolding his wings. Katrina grabbed Merlin's hand, clutching it so hard that his bones crunched.

Desmond flexed the shimmering leathery skin that was stretched tight between his purple bones. Like a bat's, thought Katrina. And then she was too scared to think anything. Her mind was full of blank white terror.

With a single powerful beat, Desmond lifted smoothly off the ground. His claws brushed the treetops. Another beat and they were at roof level, skimming over the chimneys of Whitehall. One more and they soared over the Houses of Parliament, sweeping past the face of Big Ben. Desmond circled as he climbed up and up, relentlessly spiralling heavenwards.

Katrina looked down, and then wished she hadn't. It was an amazing view, certainly. Much better than the one from the London Eye that people queued up to see. But, oh, how she hated heights!

Once he was above the rooftops, Desmond seemed to accelerate. It was as if he had opened up the throttle. Katrina felt the surge of power and realized how much he had been holding back until then: if he'd taken off at full strength he would have blasted the roof off Westminster Abbey.

Katrina shut her eyes, but it made her feel even dizzier. She swallowed and swallowed, hoping desperately that she wasn't going to be sick.

They circled higher and higher, until at last London was no more than a dark blob and the Thames was a sparkling silver thread winding through it.

Then Katrina's attention was taken up by what was above them, rather than the ever receding view of London below.

She heard it first: a crackling screaming roar. It was like a distant train at first, or an aeroplane, but the sound intensified rapidly. In the throb of a heartbeat it was deafening.

Then Katrina felt the heat. She looked up.

Bearing down on them with terrifying speed was a burning ball of rock. It was the size of a house. A very large house. A mansion. A block of flats. A skyscraper.

It's bigger than the Prime Minister said it would be, was all she had time to think, before Desmond swerved sharply away from the fireball. Then he turned and dived down after it.

Air screamed past Katrina's ears. Her eyes streamed. Her nose started to run.

Merlin was muttering, holding both hands out, fingertips outstretched. "Flaming fireball cease to be!"

Purple sparks of light shot out of the ends of his fingers. Katrina smelt the now familiar smell of burnt-out fireworks for a split second before the wind whipped it behind them.

The fire on the rock was extinguished.

Now it was only a lump of rock the size of a skyscraper hurtling towards London.

"That's no good!" said Katrina.

Desmond dived after it. They were much lower now. Katrina could just make out the buildings below.

Merlin tried again.

He held out both hands. "Be gone," he ordered. "Fragment. Disintegrate."

Purple sparks hit the rock and there was an almighty explosion. Katrina ducked as pieces of rock flew through the air.

Merlin had succeeded – to an extent. The rock the size of a skyscraper was now a million small rocks. He'd done enough to prevent global catastrophe, perhaps, but each rock was large enough to kill someone.

They had now dived down low enough to see the people below. Everyone had trooped out of the Abbey after the ceremony and was watching what they took to be an unusual daylight firework display.

"Katrinapicket," shouted Merlin desperately. "HELP!"

"What can I do?" she screamed.

"Imagine something harmless. Order the rock to become it. Do it with conviction, Katrinapicket. You have power. Use it!"

Katrina didn't have time to question Merlin's command. Katrina didn't have time to think anything. Some deep instinct took over. They both extended their hands, focussed their minds and…

"SNAPDRAGONS!" cried Katrina.

"MARMALADE!" shouted Merlin.

And so the Queen, the Prime Minister, every politician in the land, pop stars, film stars, television stars, famous footballers with their supermodel wives, Arthur, Guinevere, Lancelot and 150 knights in shining armour, including Mordred, were first doused with marmalade and then covered with snapdragons.

The snapdragons stuck beautifully to the marmalade. It made a very unusual sight.

There was a sharp intake of breath from the crowd. A moment's chilly silence.

Then the Queen started to giggle helplessly. "Flaars," she spluttered. "Ixtraordinirry flaars!"

Soon everyone was laughing.

As Desmond came in to land, there was cheering

and shouting and clapping – an uproar such as London rarely sees.

They weren't clapping the Queen. They weren't even clapping Arthur.

They were clapping Desmond. And Merlin.

And they were clapping Katrina.

"Need help from little girls, now, do you, Merlin?" sneered a slimy voice. "You must be losing your grip. It's pathetic. Utterly pathetic."

"Mordred," Merlin nodded in greeting.

Katrina shuddered, but Merlin seemed surprisingly cheerful.

Desmond cleared his throat. He stepped forward and whispered something in Merlin's ear. Merlin smiled and nodded.

"Mordred," Merlin said happily, "do you have any idea what day it is?"

Mordred looked puzzled, but said nothing.

"It's Wednesday, Mordred," Merlin continued. "You remember what happens on Wednesdays, don't you?"

Mordred frowned and tried hard to recall what special significance Wednesdays might have…

Suddenly he did. He looked at Desmond. Desmond gave him a friendly little wave. Mordred screamed. Stepped back. Turned to run.

Too late.

Desmond took half a step forward, lowered his huge head and swallowed Mordred in one gulp, as easily as a bird swallows a grasshopper.

And the Queen – thinking it was the fabulous finale to a quaite ixtraodinirry morning – clapped her hands and called out, "Will dun. Nivver sin inything laike it. Jolly good shaiw!"

The party that followed went on well into the night. The Prime Minister had organized live bands, and food, and street theatre in Hyde Park. It was fantastic. Thousands of people, with marmalade and snapdragons in their hair, ate, drank and were very, very merry.

Desmond lay on his back, legs in the air, snoozing happily. Little puffs of smoke drifted from his nostrils from time to time.

"Great animatronics," said one passer-by.

"Isn't it amazing what they can do these days?" agreed another.

*   *   *

The Prime Minister was delighted with the way everything had passed off.

"Well done. Well done," he said heartily, shaking Merlin enthusiastically by the hand. Then he patted Katrina on the head again, and went off to talk to more important people.

"I think I liked him better when he was depressed," said Katrina.

Arthur had passed the crown back to the Queen as soon as the Royal Assent had been given. There'd been no bloodshed, and no one any the wiser to the danger they'd been in.

"They all think it was just a bit of fun, don't they?" said Katrina, watching a particularly merry group of teachers paddling in the Serpentine.

"Yes," said Merlin wisely. "But better your way than mine, Katrinapicket." He shuddered as he remembered his vision of Arthur and all his knights shot dead. "You did very well."

They sat together under a large oak tree, and Katrina absent-mindedly began pulling up blades of grass. Something was bothering her. "You said I

155

was a sorceress…" Katrina said. "I'm not, am I?"

"Well … actually," Merlin replied, "yes … I believe you are. It's what drew you to me in the first place. You fell up, didn't you? Magic attracts magic, you see. Desmond knew you were special right away."

"Is *that* what you were talking about?" asked Katrina, feeling as if a great weight had suddenly been lifted from her shoulders. "That day we found him outside the art gallery… I thought he wanted to eat me."

"Good heavens, no!" said Merlin. "Did you really think that? Gracious! No, Desmond has had Mordred labelled as dragon fodder for centuries."

"So what *were* you talking about?"

"Ah… Desmond thinks I should train you properly. Says you seem a lot more sensible than Nimue ever was." Merlin flushed uncomfortably. "And he's right, of course. But I thought I'd have a little holiday first. Promised Desmond we'd see a bit of the world before I take on a new apprentice."

They looked at Desmond. The grass was singed where he'd been snoring.

"No one seems to mind him, do they?" said

Merlin. "It's astonishing. People used to be so scared of dragons…"

"They don't know he's real," explained Katrina. "They all think he's a model. A clever special effect. He won't need to pretend to be a statue again. You can pass him off as a robot."

"Yes," said Merlin with satisfaction. "Things are looking up for Desmond."

"What will happen to Arthur and his knights?" asked Katrina. "Do they have to go back to sleep?"

"Oh, no," said Merlin. "Not yet, anyway. They all deserve a bit of a break, I think. Arthur, Lancelot and Guinevere are going to go and try their luck in California. They were talking to one of those American reporters. It seems that people won't mind their unusual living arrangements there. And without Mordred to spoil things, they should be very happy… Speaking of which, here they come."

Arthur, Lancelot and Guinevere were walking across the grass towards them.

"A glorious day's work, young squire. Did I not say you had a courageous heart?" Guinevere's eyes shone with joy as she kissed Katrina gently on the forehead.

"Her bravery is greater than that of all the knights of the fellowship," added Lancelot. "Her courage soared above the clouds!"

Katrina beamed at him. It wasn't so much what he *said*, Katrina realized, as the laughter that bubbled within his words. He spread delight like a contagious disease.

And then there was Arthur.

Arthur said nothing. He simply smiled, and Katrina's heart seemed to stop beating altogether for a moment. Pride was written large on his face. He nodded his approval. Katrina flushed. Then she met his eyes and grinned back.

There was so much that could be said that in the end they hardly spoke at all. They sat in companionable silence, enjoying the warmth of the summer night, marvelling at the events of the last few days that had led them all to this moment.

But at last it started to get cold. Katrina shivered, and the spell of their charmed circle was broken. People were drifting away from the park to the warmth of their beds.

"Time to get you home, Katrinapicket," said Merlin.

Guinevere whispered something to Arthur.

He nodded. "Yes," he agreed. "It is time." He looked at Katrina. "Kneel, young squire," he commanded.

Katrina knelt obediently, wondering what on earth was happening, but feeling too tired to mind much. She felt a brief moment of surprise when Arthur drew his sword. The cold weight of metal pressed down first on one shoulder, then the other.

Arthur's voice was as rich as melted chocolate when he said, "Arise! Sir Katrinapicket."

Unfreezing Mum
(Thursday morning)

Katrina was still glowing happily when Desmond landed in the park opposite her house. The sun was up. It was Thursday morning.

"I'll wait for you here," Desmond told Merlin. "Goodbye, Sir Katrinapicket." Desmond gave Katrina a warm, smoky, scaly kiss on the cheek.

She hugged his neck but couldn't speak.

Then Merlin led her indoors.

Mum and Adrian were still in the kitchen, exactly as they had left them.

Dad had pinned a note on Mum.

"Dear Kat," it said. "Hope the Danger has passed and you are safe. Please return Mum to normal by the time I get home. I can't cope with much more of this. Love Dad."

Katrina removed the note.

She and Merlin looked at each other. There was a choked silence.

"I'll be back to train you," Merlin promised. "You shall be my apprentice, Sir Katrinapicket. You'll make a very good one, too."

"Thanks," Katrina said in a very high voice. Then, "Erm ... Merlin ... won't Mum and Adrian notice that they've lost a couple of days?"

"No, no," he assured her. "He's just come back from foreign parts, hasn't he? And she's doing something peculiar to the garden?"

Katrina nodded.

"Easy to lose track of time. They may be a little puzzled, but nothing serious."

Katrina and Merlin hugged each other fondly, said goodbye, and then Katrina took her place where she had been standing before Mum froze.

Mum had been in the middle of a sentence: "If

you ever come near Katrina again, I'll …"

Merlin waved his hands. Purple sparks flew through the air.

"… have you locked up before you can say 'Abracadabra'," yelled Mum. "Out of here… Out! OUT!" She bustled Merlin ahead of her up the hallway. "I thought I'd opened that," she said to herself, as she found the front door shut. She pulled it open again, and pushed Merlin out of the house.

On the front doorstep, he bowed low and said, "I thank you, Lady Mymum, for your gracious hospitality."

Before he had finished his sentence the door had slammed shut.

Mum stormed back into the kitchen. She looked at the clock. "It's getting late," she said, horrified. "I don't know where the time goes some days." She sniffed and stared at Katrina. "Have you been playing with fireworks, young lady?"

Adrian spat tea all over the table. He had been frozen with a cup halfway to his mouth and he had just taken a sip.

"Yuck!" he said. "It's stone cold!"

"Don't be silly," Mum snapped. "I've only just made it." She turned to Katrina and said with satisfaction. "Well, that's the last we'll see of that Merlin character."

But Sir Katrina Picket knew different.

It's Katrina Picket's birthday and not only has her favourite bear been burnt to a crisp, but her best friend's ignoring her and their supply teacher is none other than Morgan le Fay, the most evil sorceress that ever lived! Katrina summons Merlin. But can he train her to become a sorceress in time to defeat Morgan and save the country from destruction?

When Jake Jellicoe signs up as cabin boy aboard the *Flounder*, Captain Dreadnought promises him a share of the loot. But he soon discovers that the captain isn't all that he seems, and before he knows it Jake is caught up in a race for the Dread Pirate Redbeard's treasure!

Har-har me hearties!

June Crebbin

Jumping Beany

It's Pony Day at Merryfield Hall Riding School and, for the first time ever, Dad has promised to come and watch Amber jump. Everything will be perfect … as long as Amber gets to ride her favourite pony, Beany. But Donna wants to ride Beany too – and, as the jumping competition gets closer, it looks like she'll go to any lengths to get her own way!

Judy
MOOdy
was in a
mood. Not a
good mood. A
bad mood.

Megan McDonald illustrated by Peter H. Reynolds

Get in the Judy Moody mood!

Bad moods, good moods, even back-to-school moods – Judy has them all! But when her new teacher gives the class a "Me" collage project, Judy has so much fun she nearly forgets to be moody!

Meet Judy, her little "bother" Stink, her best friend Rocky and her "pest" friend Frank Pearl. They're sure to put you in a very Judy Moody mood!

When Sherlock Holmes goes missing in sinister circumstances, only his gang of young detectives can save him.

Who are the mysterious Irishmen lurking in Baker Street?

Is the dastardly Moriarty involved?

The baffling clues are about as clear as the pea-souper that cloaks London – join Wiggins, Sparrow, Queenie and the gang as they piece them together.

New pupils are made to sign their names in blood...
The assistant headmaster has no reflection...
The French teacher disappears whenever there's a
full moon... Groosham Grange, David Eliot's new
school, is a very weird place indeed!

"One of the funniest books of the year."
  Young Telegraph

"Hilarious ... speeds along at full tilt from page to
page."
  Books for Keeps

*If you've enjoyed reading this book,
look out for...*

Short novels for fluent readers